归舟：
中国元明清诗选

VOYAGE HOME:
POEMS FROM THE YUAN AND
MING AND QING DYNASTIES OF CHINA

王守义　编选
Selected and Edited by
Wang Shouyi

王守义　约翰·诺弗尔　译
Translated by
Wang Shouyi and John Knoepfle

黑龙江大学出版社
HEILONGJIANG UNIVERSITY PRESS
哈尔滨

图书在版编目（CIP）数据

　　归舟：中国元明清诗选 / 王守义编选；王守义，
（美）约翰.诺弗尔（John Knoepfle）译. -- 哈尔滨：
黑龙江大学出版社，2018.11（2020.7 重印）
　　ISBN 978-7-5686-0260-0

　　Ⅰ．①归… Ⅱ．①王… ②约… Ⅲ．①古典诗歌－诗
集－中国－元代－汉、英②古典诗歌－诗集－中国－明清
时代－汉、英 Ⅳ．① I222

　　中国版本图书馆CIP数据核字（2018）第166594号

归舟：中国元明清诗选
GUIZHOU:ZHONGGUO YUAN MING QING SHIXUAN
王守义　　编选
王守义　　约翰·诺弗尔　　译

责任编辑　陈　欣　王艳萍
出版发行　黑龙江大学出版社
地　　址　哈尔滨市南岗区学府三道街 36 号
印　　刷　哈尔滨市石桥印务有限公司
开　　本　880 毫米 ×1230 毫米　1/32
印　　张　10.875
字　　数　234 千
版　　次　2018 年 11 月第 1 版
印　　次　2020 年 7 月第 3 次印刷
书　　号　ISBN 978-7-5686-0260-0
定　　价　39.00 元

本书如有印装错误请与本社联系更换。

江村霜葉詩中画晓
峯畑樹乍生寒
戊辰仲冬月
守義先生雅鑒
溥任

溥任创作的山水画

溥任在画上的题诗

江村霜叶诗中画

晓峰烟树乍生寒

戊辰仲冬月

守义先生雅鉴

溥任

A Poem on the Painting
written by Pu Ren

like a painting so well created in a poem

frost colors the leaves in the river village

peaks at dawn and trees in the haze this morning

suddenly I shiver in the chilly air

The eleventh month in the lunar calendar, 1988

To Mr. Wang Shouyi

By Pu Ren

此照摄于 2012 年 5 月,美国伊利诺伊州春田市。
This photo was taken in Springfield, Illinois, USA in May, 2012.

作 者 简 介
About the Authors

王守义于 1942 年生于中国辽宁省大连市,祖籍为山东省牟平县(现烟台市牟平区)。毕业于黑龙江大学英语语言文学专业,后在美国伊利诺伊大学完成美国文学专业硕士学位。

他曾为黑龙江大学学术委员会委员、英语系教授、美国文学专业研究生导师,曾担任英语系主任、美国研究所所长、外语学院副院长。

他曾于 1996 年至 1997 年应邀作为富布莱特驻美国学者（跨文化影响项目）任教于阿什兰大学英语系；后曾在伊利诺伊大学春田分校的国际研究中心任客座教授，在休斯敦大学亚裔美国人文化研究中心任客座研究员。

他曾任中国全国美国文学研究会副会长、中国跨文化交际学会常务理事、中国美国学学会理事、中国英语教学研究会理事、黑龙江省作家协会会员、《诗林》杂志特约编辑。

他曾以作者、合作者，译者、合译者，编者、合编者的身份在中国和美国出版十九本著作，包括他自己的诗集《风的愿望》。他曾撰写三十余篇论文，其中多篇发表在国家级学术刊物上，如《中国比较文学》《外国语》《外国文学评论》《求是学刊》《外语学刊》《文艺评论》《伊利诺伊评论》等。

他为七本出版著作撰写了序言，在中国、美国、韩国的研讨会上发表二十余篇论文。此外，他的多篇诗作、文艺杂谈、译诗、短篇小说翻译、书评见于多种报纸和刊物上。

他现在是加拿大文学翻译家协会顶级会员，与妻子孙苏荔住在加拿大橡树岭，与邦德湖和威尔考克斯湖为邻。夏天，他喜欢在湖上划他的独木舟 —— 湍流号；冬天，他喜欢在覆雪的山林小路上散步。

Wang Shouyi was born in Dalian City, Liaoning Province, China in 1942. His hometown is Muping County (now Muping District of Yantai City), Shandong Province, China. He graduated from Heilongjiang University with a major in English Language and Literature. Later he earned his Master Degree in American Literature at the University of Illinois Springfield (UIS).

At Heilongjiang University, he worked as a member of the Academic Committee of Heilongjiang University, a professor of the English department, an advisor for graduate students of American Literature, chairman of the English department, director of the Institute of American Studies and vice-dean of the Foreign Languages Institute.

As a Fulbright Professor in Residence in the USA on the Cross-Cultural Influence Program 1996–1997, he taught in the English department, Ashland University, and later he served as a visiting professor teaching in the International Studies Centre at the UIS and also as a visiting researcher in the Asian American Cultural Studies Centre of University of Houston.

He was the vice-president of the China Association for the Study of American Literature, a standing council member of the China Association for Intercultural Communication, a council member of the China Association for American Studies, a council member of the China English Language Education Association. He was also a member of the Heilongjiang Writers Association and a special editor of the magazine

Poetry Forest.

His nineteen books have been published in China and the USA, of which he is as author or co-author, translator or co-translator, editor or co-editor. He also published the collection of his own poems — *The Wind's Will.* He has more than thirty essays, some of which appeared in nationally prestigious academic journals such as *Comparative Literature in China, Journal of Foreign Languages, Foreign Literature Review, Seeking Truth, Foreign Language Research, Literature and Art Criticism, Illinois Issues* and so on.

He also wrote seven prefaces for his and other authors' books. He has more than twenty papers presented at symposiums in China, the USA and South Korea. His poems, literary articles, translated poems, translated short stories and book reviews have been published in newspapers and magazines.

He is currently a full member of the Literary Translators' Association of Canada and lives with his wife Sun Suli at Oak Ridges close to Bond Lake and Lake Wilcox in Canada. He likes paddling his canoe "Speed River" in the lakes in summer and hiking on the snow-covered trails in the wooded hills in winter.

约翰·诺弗尔于 1923 年生于美国俄亥俄州辛辛那提市。二战期间，他服役于美国海军，在登陆艇部队任初级军官，在太平洋战争中曾运送第五海军陆战队登陆硫磺岛。在登岛作战时，他的双腿被弹片击中。伤愈后，他又参加运送二十二军登陆冲绳岛，伤势复发，军旅生涯结束。仍然存留在他的双腿里的炮弹碎片还能让他想起那个死里逃生的太平洋之夜。

1956 年，他结束了在辛辛那提的教育电视节目的工作，开始在俄亥俄州立大学、南伊利诺伊大学教英语。后来他又先后在玛丽维尔大学和圣路易斯大学担任英语和文学写作两门课的助教。从 1972 年到退休，他一直在伊利诺伊大学担任英国文学和文学写作教授。

他出版了约二十本诗集，其中包括《流入岛屿的河流》（芝加哥大学出版社，1965 年），《来自桑格蒙的诗》（伊利诺伊大学出版社，1985 年），《求赦免》（德瑞德出版社，1994 年），《抗饥荒的祈祷和其他爱尔兰诗歌》（堪萨斯市密苏里大学，BkMk 出版社，2004 年），《黄昏的芦荟》（印第安画笔诗人出版社，2015 年），还有各种学术论文和书评。1986 年，他曾因对中西部文学的杰出贡献获马克·吐温奖，同年获伊利诺伊年度优秀作家奖，2012 年在春田获市长艺术奖。

1985 年，他与王守义合作翻译了《唐诗选》和《宋诗词选》，由美国匙河诗歌出版社出版精装本和平装本，责任编辑是大卫·R.皮卡斯基。这两本书后于 1989 年由中国黑龙江人民出版社出版精装合订本《唐宋诗词英译》，责任编辑是李向东。他与王守义全力合作，每当完成共同满意的一行翻译，就会有成就感。约翰在翻译的过程中,对中国的诗歌、历史和文化产生了由衷的敬意。他还和罗伯特·布莱、詹姆斯·赖特合作翻译诗歌,出版了《凯撒·乌莱侯的二十首诗》。这些诗后来收进《聂鲁达和乌莱侯》一书中,由比肯出版社在 1971 年出版,此书在 1993 年再版。

他现在与妻子佩姬·诺弗尔住在伊利诺伊州春田市。他喜欢在一些场合给朋友和家人吹奏口琴。有时,在落雨的下午,他喜欢在电脑上尝试敲出几行好诗。

John Knoepfle was born in Cincinnati, Ohio, USA in 1923. He served in the Navy in World War Two as an officer in the Amphibious Corps, in the Pacific War, making assault landings for the 5th Marines at Iwo Jima and he was struck by a shell burst. After recovering, he joined the assault landing for the 22nd Army on Okinawa Island. But the injury reopened which ultimately brought an end to his military career. The shrapnel in his legs is still a reminder of his narrow escape that night in the Pacific.

In 1956 his educational television career in Cincinnati ended and he began his career as an instructor in English at Ohio State University and Southern Illinois University. He served as an assistant professor of English and Creative Writing at Maryville University and later at Saint Louis University. From 1972 until his retirement, he was a professor of

English Literature and Creative Writing at the University of Illinois Springfield.

He has published some twenty books of poems including *Rivers into Islands* (University of Chicago Press, 1965), *Poems from the Sangamon* (University of Illinois Press, 1985), *Begging an Amnesty* (The Druid Press, 1994), *Prayer Against Famine and other Irish Poems* (BkMk Press, University of Missouri, Kansas City, 2004)and *The Aloe of Evening* (Indian Paintbrush Poets, 2015). Awards include the Mark Twain Award for Distinguished Contributions to Midwestern Literature in 1986, Illinois Excellent Author of the Year in 1986, Mayor's Awards for the Arts, in Springfield in 2012.

He began working together with Wang Shouyi and published the translations of *Tang Dynasty Poems* and *Song Dynasty Poems* in hardback and paperback which were published by Spoon River Poetry Press in 1985, David R. Pichaske was the editor. These books were combined into one — *Poems from Tang and Song Dynasties* in hardback in 1989 which was published by Heilongjiang People's Publishing House, Li Xiangdong was the editor. John and Shouyi shared hard work and a sense of achievement whenever they agreed on a good line. And John gained a serious respect for Chinese poetry, history and culture. He also translated poems with Robert Bly and James Wright and published in the book *Twenty Poems of Cesar Vallejo*. Those poems were reprinted in *Neruda and Vallejo* by Beacon Press in 1971 and republished in 1993.

He lives with his wife Peggy Knoepfle in Springfield, Illinois. He enjoys playing the harmonica for friends and family on occasion. And sometimes he likes to try striking a few good lines on his computer on a rainy afternoon.

前 言

1985年，美国匙河诗歌出版社出版了《唐诗选》和《宋诗词选》的英译本，这两本书得到伊利诺伊州艺术委员会和（美国）国家艺术支援会的部分资助。这两本书是我在1983年至1985年留美期间与美国著名诗人约翰·诺弗尔合作翻译的。在这以后，我开始问自己，从中国唐朝到清朝的古典诗歌翻译工程何时才能完成。

现在，黑龙江大学出版社将于2018年在中国哈尔滨出版这本书：《归舟：中国元明清诗选》。整个翻译计划终于完成。

在出版这本书的时候，黑龙江大学出版社还决定同时出版《江雪：中国唐宋诗词选》，把以前在美国出版的两本书（后来由黑龙江人民出版社于1989年出版了合订本）中的全部译诗收入其中。我是在1988年把在美国出版的两本书合编成一本，以使其进入中国图书市场的。合编此书时，我加进了两首宋诗，原稿也是由我与约翰·诺弗尔合作翻译的。

这个决定使两本书成为一个系列，这才有可能呈现中国古典诗歌从开始到结束历经了唐、宋、元、明、清各个朝代的完整轨迹。我和约翰·诺弗尔都对黑龙江大学出版社怀揣感激，感激他们的善良和远见让这一出版盛事成为可能。

在《唐诗选》和《宋诗词选》这两本英译著作在美国出版十年之后，在合订本《唐宋诗词英译》在中国出版6年之后，我与约翰在伊利诺伊大学的春田校园相遇,那时我来美国参加伊利诺伊州立大学的建校周年庆典活动。在这一周的停留时间里,我告诉诺弗尔教授,我们的译作在中国得到了好评。评论发表在由黑龙江大学主办的《外语学刊》上,来自一些重要的学者、教授及著名文学翻译家。其中一篇评论文章来自著名文学翻译家赵辛而,题目是《从两部英译古诗集看近年来古诗英译之趋势》,刊登在1986年第4期。另外一篇评论文章是由德高望重的教授李锡胤所撰,题目是《从李清照〈如梦令〉英译文谈起》,登在1992年第3期上。还有一些好评,它们来自"王守义、诺弗尔《唐宋诗词英译》讨论会",由黑龙江省翻译工作者协会和《外语学刊》编辑部共同发起举办,参加的人有知名的教授、文学翻译家、文学翻译批评家和语言学家。讨论会上的评论经由《外语学刊》的编辑王德庆先生详细报道,题目是《一次关于中国古诗词英译的讨论》,该评论刊登在《外语学刊》1992年第3期。同时,约翰·诺弗尔也给我介绍了他在图书馆、书店和学校朗读这些译诗时所得到的热烈的反响和好评。我和约翰都颇受鼓舞,跃跃欲试去完成这个计划的后一半,向全世界说英语的人展示中国文化的瑰宝。分享这些诗歌就是我们的动力之源。

后来我似乎又有机会与约翰一起开展工作了,因为我应邀参加富布赖特项目——"富布赖特驻美国学者从1996年至1997年的跨文化影响项目",在俄亥俄州的阿什兰德大学英语系讲四门课程,同时在其他几所大学做讲座。实际上我只是与约翰见了几次面而已,因为每次单程要开一天的车。显然,我无法开始这个计划。我和约翰都认为我们需要面对面地一起工作,这样两个诗人可以彼此交谈,彼此聆听,这样在翻译过程中我们才能彼此理解,彼此欣赏。尽管如此，我还是找出时间开始了翻译中国元明清诗的先期准备。

那时诺弗尔教授已经出版了十五本自己的诗集，我只出版了一本中文诗集，我的一些诗发表在报纸副刊和文学刊物上。我也曾担任过《诗林》杂志的特约编辑。

尽管如此，那一年还是很有收获的一年，因为我有机会与美国非常有才能的青年诗人、英语教授史蒂芬·黑文一起工作，他后来去了波士顿的莱斯利大学写作硕士研究生院担任院长。我们花费很多时间翻译了朦胧派诗人顾城和芒克的作品。后来，其中的一些译诗发表在美国的一些文学刊物上，例如《两线》《奇盾》《后果杂志》等。全部的译诗共计四十六首已被收进一本中国当代诗歌选集里，一家美国出版社正计划出版此书。

第二年我到伊利诺伊大学做客座教授，还是讲四门课，不过是在国际研究中心。这样我就又可以与约翰·诺弗尔翻译中国古典诗词了。这次我们翻译的是中国元朝、明朝和清朝的诗。在那个学年里，我们完成了第一稿，计划向前推进了一大步。

元朝部分，我从十四位诗人的诗里选了二十四首诗；明朝部分，我从二十一位诗人的诗里选了二十六首诗；清朝部分，我从三十三位诗人的诗里选了五十一首诗。我从清朝选的诗多于从元朝或明朝选的诗是因为，事实上，由于蒙古族击垮宋朝并建立政权，诗歌的写作转入低谷。元朝只持续了一百六十多年，很多诗人随之进入明朝。我们很难从中划出一条线来分开两个朝代的诗。此外，明朝在建立初年和末年都经历了很多动荡和变革，诗歌写作也在某种程度上受到干扰。不过，这本书并不比《江雪：中国唐宋诗词选》容量小，因为这本书里选了好几首篇幅长、内容复杂的诗。

时间的跨度非常大，出类拔萃的诗人又这么多，他们又来自不同的朝代、不同的地域，代表多种多样的诗歌写作流派，从中选择诗作非常困难。不但要选著名诗人和其广为流传的诗作，还要选择具有丰富文化色彩的诗作，这是非常具有挑战性的。我尝试选择不同类型的诗作，不仅有描写上层社会生活甚至宫廷王室生活的诗，还要有描写普通人生活甚至农夫的生活的诗。在这本书里，体现了巨大的社会变革，特别是具有几千年历史的封建社会在1911年的终结。我希望我选的诗作能给读者更好地展示那几个朝代的诗歌面貌，更好地展现在那触目惊心的社会演变中诗人的情感的复杂层面。

　　我在挑选诗歌时，特别在意让中国文化在世界上更好地被了解。这就是我特意选择了这些难以翻译的诗作的原因，它们充满了神话、传说、历史、文化故事以及民间故事和典故。这些在一首即使是很短的古典诗里，都是很容易操作的，可是在翻译成英文时可就得用尽浑身解数了。而好处是这类诗歌负载着众多的文化的传说、意象、象征和内涵，在促成跨文化交际和不同文化的融汇方面是具有强大冲击力的。我选择了一些这类诗歌，因为我相信目的语读者会非常高兴通过读诗了解其他文化的形态和精髓。一旦两种文化得到连接，人们就会在相互理解、合作和交流中感到舒适。

　　我和约翰仍然需要一年的时间完成第二稿和第三稿的修订。当我们注意到，经过多年后，我们之间相隔的距离越来越远了，已经没有可能经常会面时，我们开始通过网络、电话、手机恢复了我们的工作。这种方式需要花更多的时间，需要面对更多的困难，但是我们坚持这样工作多年，直到我们完成了第三稿。这个过程令人愉快。

考虑到中国古诗词大量用典会造成很多理解障碍，我决定使用注释，帮助读者移走在探索诗歌意义过程中的羁绊。注释只是与历史、地理、文化相关。注释在解读和欣赏诗歌方面不提供任何暗示和建议。我们把欣赏艺术的使命完全留给伟大的读者。尽管如此，我和约翰还是尽量译出那些典故的内涵，这样读者甚至可能得到认识上的震撼，被诗的艺术所感染，在读那些注释之前就进入欣赏状态。我在书中采用了重复加注释的做法，因为读者很可能偶然打开这本选集，只读其中一首诗。在这种情况下，读者还要去找前面另一首诗中的相同注释，就会干扰欣赏的状态。而重复注释给读者省去这个麻烦，使读者能专注于诗歌欣赏。

这本书里，诗人出现的顺序的安排原则和在《江雪：中国唐宋诗词选》中的原则相同。先出生的诗人被排在前面，同年出生的诗人中先谢世的被排在前面，那些生卒年代告缺的诗人尽量被排在最后面，等下一次再版，那时我们或许会有这项信息。

这本书的书名包含收在本书内的揭傒斯的一首诗的题目——《归舟》，这首诗在元朝颇有影响。鉴于这本书是一本中国古典诗歌的选集，我选用这个题目来反射出诗人的情感在诗歌被创作出来的文化中，在诗歌受到钟爱的历史中，在诗歌得到爱护、流传的时代变迁中所起到的重要作用。在中国古典诗歌中，家总是人类情感的标志，而回家也永远是人类生活的一个主题。我喜欢这首诗，是因为诗人把他自己的人生苦难放进这样一个美丽的自然环境中。虽然他知道在家乡他将因自己的失败而感到羞愧，他还是情不自禁地赞赏眼前的美景。诗人对自然的爱和他在回家的路上的情怀深深地打动了我。对于那些悲悯的诗人来说,回家总是一件让人心碎的事情。我觉得《归舟》是中国古时候那些回乡诗中不同凡响的一首。

我喜欢中国古典诗歌,也练习写这种形式的诗歌,还填填词。这种练习帮我更好地理解那些在遥远的过去写这样的诗的诗人。每当我阅读这些诗的时候,我就感到能更多地了解中国传统文化。这些让我思考很多。当我背诵一两首诗,陷入沉思时,我总是设法说服自己,如果我持续沉思下去,就会掌握中国文化的错综复杂,仿佛其密码就藏身在那些诗里。我希望我的读者也会有这样的体验。我抱着希望等待听到您读诗的反馈。

作为这本书的插图的画作是著名画家和书法家溥任(1918—2015)赠送给我的礼物。他是中国末代皇帝溥仪的弟弟。鉴于这本选集截止于1911年,也就是清朝结束的一年,因此我很看重在这本书里与读者分享这幅画的重要意义,何况这是一份个人礼物,从未向公众展示。再者,溥任先生去世只在几年之前,我想与读者分享这幅画,使它也成为对溥任的纪念。

我和约翰都感谢黑龙江大学出版社的总编辑刘剑刚先生。没有他的智慧和判断,这本书和这个图书系列是不可能完成的。他善意的帮助、坚定的支持及巨大的耐心是我们工作的最大保证。

我们也要感谢责任编辑陈欣、王艳萍,感谢她们对这个项目的认真关切和为书稿所做的辛苦工作。

我们也从心底感谢徐文培教授,感谢他在学术上的支持。

我和约翰要特别感谢佩姬·诺弗尔夫人和孙苏荔女士,感谢她们始终不渝的关心、支持和帮助。

我们还要感谢洛赞妮·福莱特女士和宜森·兰姆先生,感谢他们在校读中的帮助和建议。

我们真诚地希望我们会收到读者的建议和矫正,那将给我们机会润饰我们的翻译。提前感谢您的善意。

王守义

2017 年 6 月

于多伦多教堂街

(本文翻译:翠西·世爽·梅　校订:王守义)

Preface

I started asking myself when John Knoepfle and I would finish the project of Translating Classical Chinese Poems from the Tang Dynasty to the Qing Dynasty (618 AD-1911 AD) after the two books of English translation — *Tang Dynasty Poems* and *Song Dynasty Poems* — were published in the United States of America in 1985 by Spoon River Poetry Press, funded in part by the Illinois Arts Council and the National Endowment for Arts. John Knoepfle is a well-known American poet, with whom I completed these two books in collaboration during my stay in the United States from 1983 to 1985.

Now at last this book can be presented: *Voyage Home: Poems from the Yuan and Ming and Qing Dynasties of China*, published by Heilongjiang University Press in Harbin, China, in 2018.

When it was determined to publish the above book, Heilongjiang University Press made another decision to republish the second book: *Snow on the River: Poems from the Tang and Song Dynasties of China* at the same time which includes all the poems in the two books previously published in the United States, later as a combined version published by Heilongjiang People's Publishing House in Harbin, China in 1989. I compiled those two books into one book in 1988 to make it available in China's book market. I added to this combined version two poems of the Song Dynasty, which were also translated through my collaboration with John Knoepfle.

This decision made it possible to have this series present the whole course of classical Chinese Poetry from beginning to end through the Tang, Song, Yuan, Ming and Qing Dynasties of China. John and I owe many thanks to Heilongjiang University Press for their kindness and brilliant idea to make this happen.

Ten years after the two books of English translations — *Tang Dynasty Poems* and *Song Dynasty Poems* — were published in the United States, and six years after the combined version — *Poems from Tang and Song Dynasties* — was published in China, I met with John at the University of Illinois at Springfield during my one-week-stay for the university's anniversary celebration. I told Professor Knoepfle that our works received favorable reviews from some very important scholars, professors and literary translators in China appearing in *Foreign Language Research* which was hosted by Heilongjiang University, one of which was a review by well-known literary translator Mr. Zhao Xin'er in the 4th issue, 1986, entitled "Review of the Trend in Translating Classical Chinese Poems into English from Reading Two Collections" and another one of which was a review by a very prestigious professor — Li Xiyin in the 3rd issue, 1992, entitled "On the English Versions of Li Qingzhao's Poem 'Rumengling'". Favorable reviews were also from the Symposium on the *English Translation of Poems from Tang and Song Dynasties* by Wang Shouyi and John Knoepfle on the initiative of Heilongjiang Translators Association and the editorial board of *Foreign Language Research* with participants of professors, celebrated literary translators, famous literary translation critics and well-known scholars of linguistics. Comments and remarks from the symposium were reported by Mr. Wang Deqing , one of the editors, which was entitled "A Discussion on the English Translation of Classical Chinese Poems" appearing in *Foreign Language Research*, in the 3rd issue, 1992. In return, John updated me on the kind responses and favorable reviews he received when he did the readings in libraries, book stores and schools. John and I felt so much encouraged to accomplish the second part of the project to display the treasures in Chinese culture to English readers all over the world. To share these poems is the source of our motivation.

Then it seemed to me I had another opportunity to work together with John when I was on the Fulbright Program: Cross-Cultural Influence as a Fulbright Scholar in Residence in USA from 1996 to 1997, teaching four courses in the English Department at Ashland University, Ashland, Ohio and shared by a few other universities. Actually, it turned out that I was only able to meet John a couple of times by driving a whole day each way. Obviously, I couldn't start the project. John and I believed that we needed to work together face to face so that two poets could talk to each other and listen to each other for the translation of a poem with mutual understanding and mutual appreciation. Even though I still had time to launch in the preparation for translation of poems from the Yuan and Ming and Qing Dynasties of China.

By then Professor Knoepfle had published almost fifteen collections of his own poems and I had published only one collection of my own Chinese poems and some of my poems appeared in newspapers and magazines. I had also served as a special editor of a poetry magazine — *Poetry Forest*.

However, that was a fruitful year because I had the great opportunity to work with Stephen Haven, a very talented young American poet and a professor of English, who later is the director of Master of Writing program in Lesley University in Boston. We were busy translating poems from mystic poets Gu Cheng and Mang Ke. Later, some of the translations appeared in American literary magazines such as *Two Lines*, *Artful Dodge* and *Consequence Magazine* and so on. All the poems translated, a total of forty-six poems, will be published in an anthology of Chinese modern poetry by an American publisher soon.

When I was teaching at the University of Illinois at Springfield the next year as a visiting professor. I still taught four courses, but at the International Studies Centre. So that I was able to work with John Knoepfle again on the translation of classical Chinese poems. This time we worked on the poems from the Yuan and Ming and Qing Dynasties of China, and we completed the first version of the translation in that academic year. That was great progress.

I selected twenty-four poems from fourteen poets in the Yuan Dynasty, twenty-six poems from twenty-one poets in the Ming Dynasty and fifty-one poems from thirty-three poets in the Qing Dynasty. I selected fewer poems from the Yuan and Ming Dynasties than from the Qing

Dynasty. As a matter of fact, due to the disturbances of the Mongol establishment after the invasion of the Song Dynasty, the composition of poetry declined. The Yuan Dynasty lasted only about one hundred and sixty years and many of the poets were actually merged into the Ming Dynasty. There are some difficulties in drawing a line between these two periods. Besides, the Ming Dynasty went through many changes in its early years and also in its later years. The composition of poetry was somewhat interrupted. However, this book is not shorter in length than *Snow on the River: Poems from the Tang and Song Dynasties of China* because quite a few long and complicated poems were selected into this collection.

It was hard to select poems from such a long time period and from so many outstanding poets in different dynasties and in different locations and from multiple styles of poetry writing. It was very challenging to choose not only the famous poets and popular poems but also some poems that have great value in revealing the culture. I tried to select different types of poems not only the ones depicting the life of the upper class, including imperial court, but also the ones about ordinary people reflecting even lives of farmers. Social changes covered in this book are tremendous, especially the ending of thousands of years of Chinese feudal society in 1911. I hope my selection will give readers a better view of the poetry in those dynasties and of the complexity of the emotions of poets in the extraordinary diversification of society.

In my selection, I paid more attention to making Chinese culture better-known to the world. That's the reason I deliberately chose these poems which are difficult to translate given that they are full of mythological, legendary, historical, cultural stories and also folklore and adaptations of other literary works, which are easy to handle even in a very short poem in Chinese but require tremendous efforts in English translation. But the good thing is that these poems carry a great deal of cultural legends, images, symbols and implications, which are powerful for cross-cultural communication and enhance the fusion of different cultures. I chose quite a few of poems because I believe the target language readers will be delighted to know the patterns and essence of other cultures through poetry. Once the connection between any two different cultures is established, people will feel much more comfortable in their mutual understanding, co-operation and interaction.

John and I needed another year to work out the revisions for the second and third version. When we noticed that the miles between our residences had extended so much after years, and there was no possibility of meeting frequently, we resumed our work through internet, telephone and cellular phone. It took much more time and it caused more difficulties, but we kept working like this for years until we finished the third version. That process was joyous.

Considering there were so many barriers in understanding caused by the many allusive quotations in classical Chinese poems, I decided to adopt notes which are designed to help remove obstacles in approaching the meaning of the poems. The notes are only related to history, geography and culture. There are no hints or suggestions in interpretation or appreciation of the poems. We leave the mission of enjoying the arts to our great readers. Even though John and I tried hard to crack these allusions so that readers can get that shock of recognition, can be touched by the art of the poems, and thus become involved in the appreciation before reading those notes. I never hesitated to add a duplicate note to a poem. I believe that a reader may open this anthology at any time to read one poem. In such a case, the joy of reading may get disturbed if the reader needs to look for a note in another page. With the help of duplicate notes, readers can enjoy more in the poetry reading.

The arrangement of the order for poets appearing in the book followed the same principal as in *Snow on the River: Poems from the Tang and Song Dynasties of China.* Those who were born earlier were listed first, but if they were born in the same year, those who died earlier were listed first. We tried to put those whose birth date and death date we lack at the end waiting for next edition if by then we have that piece of information.

In the title of this book, I used the title of a poem in this book — *Voyage Home* written by Jie Xisi who was an influential poet in the Yuan Dynasty. Since this book is an anthology of classical Chinese poems, I chose this title to reflect how the poets' emotions play an important role in the culture in which the poems were created and in the history in which the poems were loved and in the changes of dynasties in which the poems were cherished. Home is always an icon in human feelings in classical Chinese poems and returning home is forever a theme of human life. I like this poem because the poet places the miseries of his life in such a beautiful natural environment. Even though he was going to be ashamed of his failure in his hometown, he still couldn't help admiring the scene in front of him. I was deeply impressed by the poet's love of nature and his emotion while heading home. Returning home has always been a heartbreaking thing for sad poets. I assume *Voyage Home* is an extraordinary example in ancient China among poems of returning home.

I love classical Chinese poetry and I practice writing this type of poems. I also write lyrics to the classical melodies. This practice leads me to a better understanding of those who wrote poems so long ago. Whenever I read these poems I feel I know more about traditional Chinese culture. These make me think and think a lot. When I fall into deep thoughts after reciting one poem or two poems, I try to convince myself that if I keep thinking, I can grasp the intricacies of Chinese culture, if the code really lies in those poems. I hope my readers will have the same experience. I'm keeping my fingers crossed waiting to hear your response to the poems.

The painting included in this book is a gift to me from Pu Ren (1918 –2015), who was a well-known artist both in painting and in calligraphy, younger brother of the last emperor in China whose name is Pu Yi. As this collection ends in 1911 when the Qing Dynasty ended, I treasure the significance of the painting being able to share with other readers in this book. In addition, this is a personal gift and it has never been offered to the public before. Sadly, Mr. Pu Ren passed away just a few years ago. I try to share the painting with readers , that may just serve as a memorial to Pu Ren.

John and I thank Mr. Liu Jian'gang who is the editor-in-chief in Heilongjiang University Press. This book and this series of books would have been impossible without his wisdom and judgment. His kind help, firm support and great patience meant everything for our work.

We also extend our thanks to Chen Xin and Wang Yanping who are the editors for their sincere concern for this project and their hard work on the book.

Our thanks from the bottom of our hearts also go to Professor Xu Wenpei for his academic support.

John and I want to thank specially Mrs. Peggy Knoepfle and Ms. Sun Suli for their ever-lasting care, concern and help.

We also thank Ms. Rozanne Flatt and Mr. Ethan Lam for their help and suggestions in proofreading.

We sincerely look forward to receiving suggestions and even corrections from readers, which will give us a chance to improve the translation. Thanks ahead for your kindness.

Wang Shouyi

Church Street,Toronto

June, 2017

目录·Contents

元朝诗选
The Yuan Dynasty Poems
1206—1368

明朝诗选
The Ming Dynasty Poems
1368—1644

清朝诗选
The Qing Dynasty Poems
1616—1911

黄景仁 Huang Jingren (1749—1783)

张问陶 Zhang Wentao (1764—1814)

陈　沆 Chen Hang (1785—1825)

林则徐 Lin Zexu (1785—1850)

元朝诗选

The Yuan Dynasty Poems

1206—1368

博浪沙

陈 孚

一击车中胆气豪,

祖龙社稷已动摇。

如何十二金人外,

犹有人间铁未销。

Bolangsha

Chen Fu

one fierce blow struck the carriage

that warrior oh what bravery

it shook the emperor and his empire

how could this be possible after the emperor

seized the weapons of the country people

and melted them down for twelve giant statues

and yet there was a warrior

with metal enough for his own hammer

Bolangsha was a pass then in He'nan Province, where the Emperor Shihuang of the Qin Dynasty was attacked by a warrior from former Han Kingdom which was one of the six Kingdoms conquered by Shihuang for the unification of China, but the warrior struck a wrong carriage.

岳鄂王墓

赵孟頫

鄂王坟上草离离，

秋日荒凉石兽危。

南渡君臣轻社稷，

中原父老望旌旗。

英雄已死嗟何及，

天下中分遂不支。

莫向西湖歌此曲，

水光山色不胜悲。

At the Grave of Yue Fei

Zhao Mengfu

weeds are thick on the grave of Yue Fei

the bitter winds in the fall

almost topple the stone effigy

the emperor and his officials

they escaped to the south of the Yangtze River

they did not care about what was lost

people in the middle land of the country

hoped to see the banners of the Song Dynasty again

but the hero was persecuted

there is no use being sad about this

it is too late for regret

the country is divided

the south cannot hold out much longer

do not sing these lines to the West Lake

I think the hills and those waters are sad enough

there is more sorrow than they can bear

Yue Fei was the commander of army in the Song Dynasty, who fought against the invaders from the Jin Dynasty triumphantly, but was framed by those who planned to surrender and was falsely accused and executed in 1142. His grave is on the side of the West Lake.

宗阳宫望月分韵得声字

杨 载

老君台上凉如水，

坐看冰轮转二更。

大地山河微有影，

九天风露寂无声。

蛟龙并起承金榜，

鸾凤双飞载玉笙。

不信弱流三万里，

此身今夕到蓬瀛。

Enjoying the Moonlight from Zongyang Palace

Yang Zai

on Laojuntai the people are so solemn
enjoying a moonlight as cold as spring water

we sit here looking at that moon
a wheel of ice until the midnight hour

what a reflection hovers there
this mountain and this river
the mysterious landscape of the moon

the wind calms down in the late night
and you see the dew covered meadows
their absolute silence

a pair of dragons dance through banks of cloud
their backs are etched with golden names

those appointed officials as the chosen ones

immortals are playing reed pipes

on the wings of the phoenix and its mate

as they soar in the heavens

it is said the ocean around the fairy islands

on which a seagoing ship will not float

but I feel I am already in Penglai or Yingzhou

Laojuntai is in Zongyang Palace in Hangzhou. **Penglai and Yingzhou** are both the fairy islands in Chinese legend.

题渔村图

虞　集

黄叶江南何处村，

渔翁三两坐槐根。

隔溪相就一烟棹，

老妪具炊双瓦盆。

霜前渔官未竭泽，

蟹中抱黄鲤肪白。

已烹甘瓠当晨餐，

更撷寒蔬共莝席。

垂竿何人无意来，

晚风落叶何毰毢。

了无得失动微念，

况有兴亡生远哀。

忆昔采芝有园绮，

犹被留侯迫之起，

莫将名姓落人间，

随此横图卷秋水。

Lines on a Painting of a Fishing Village
Yu Ji

leaves turned yellow here in this village
somewhere south of the Yangtze River

two or three fishermen are chatting
beneath every locust tree

there is a small boat
on the far side of the creek

smoke from a cooking fire
drifts upward from the prow of the boat

an old woman there
arranges her earthenware

it is not really the season for fishing
the shiver of the first frost is yet to come

the inspectors are not here yet
they could seize all we have caught

the crabs are heavy with roe
and the flesh of carp is solid and white

the woman also cooked squash for breakfast
she has picked some greens for dinner

there is a single fisherman
he dangles a pole over the water

he is in no hurry to catch a fish
he is just passing the time

the wind rising at twilight
sends the leaves whirling around him

nothing bothers this fisherman
winning or losing in the world
it doesn't matter

the rise or fall of the Kingdom
cannot set a hook in his heart

I think of the four reclusive sages
who lived once on Shang Mountain

and how Zhang Liang helped the emperor
convince them to serve in the palace

and how this cost them their quiet lives
they would become famous

I would not want to be famous myself
and have my name bandied in this world

let my name be rolled up in the horizontal scroll
with the cold waters painted there

Two of the four sages were Dongyuangong and Qiliji, who refused the emperor's request for assistance in the Han Dynasty, but the emperor's advisor, Zhang Liang, secured their aid for the Crown Prince.

至正改元辛巳寒食日示弟及诸子侄

虞　集

江山信美非吾土，

漂泊栖迟近百年。

山舍墓田同水曲，

不堪梦觉听啼鹃。

For My Younger Brothers and Nephews
on Cold Food Day in 1341

Yu Ji

this is a beautiful land

but it is not my true home

it has been a century now

since the family came to this place

I know the hills and houses

the graves in the fields

the lakes everywhere

but when I come out of my dream

I could swear I hear the call: "go home"
it's not the time for cuckoo though

The call: "**Go home**" was in a legend about the Three Kingdoms. The king of Shu in the Sichuan Province of today turned into a cuckoo after the loss of his land, singing until his tongue bled. His singing sounds like "go home" in Chinese. Cuckoos sing in summer. **Cold Food Day** is the day before Qingming Festival. It is a festival for having cold meals only to avoid using fire in memory of a hero — Jie Zitui who was burned to death when the emperor ordered the mountain set on fire hoping to get this well-known hermit out so that he could honor him because Jie Zitui once saved the emperor's life.

听 雨

虞 集

屏风围坐鬓鬖鬖，

绛蜡摇光照暮酣。

京国多年情尽改，

忽听春雨忆江南。

Listening to the Rain

Yu Ji

here I am behind the screens
my hair has grown long and thin

the light of my red candle
flickers in the late night shadows
I have had too much to drink

I have lived in the capital
most of my life
and that made me a northern man

but suddenly the spring rain
I sit here listening to the rain

it reminds me of my home town
south of the Yangtze River

送欣上人笑隐住龙翔寺

萨都剌

江南隐者人不识，

一日声名动九重。

地湿厌看天竺雨，

月明来听景阳钟。

衲衣香暖留春麝，

石钵云寒卧夜龙。

何日相从陪杖履，

秋风江上采芙蓉。

Saying Goodbye to Monk Xiao Yin
Who Will be in Charge of Longxiang Temple

Sa Dula

he was our own hermit

lived south of the Yangtze River

and no one knew him

and then suddenly he was famous

all over the world

it was the emperor himself

who summoned him

and he must have been tired

watching it raining here

and the earth around Tianzhu Temple

so sodden underfoot

he will surely be happy

hearing the Jingyang bell

sounding awash in moonlight

on our damp mornings in spring

his robes will be scented with aromatic fires

and when he gives his homilies at night in the fall

there will be cold smoke from his stone bowl

oh he will send a dragon down the spines

of those who are listening

I think I would be fortunate

if I could be his follower there

we will gather the lotus blossoms

on the river in the autumn winds

Xiao Yin was released from the Tianzhu Temple in Hangzhou and appointed to be in charge of the Longxiang Temple in Nanjing by Emperor Wenzong in 1328, in the Yuan Dynasty. **Jingyang Bell** was a huge bell made in the imperial court of the south Dynasty in Jinling (Nanjing). The bell got its name of Jingyang Tower, into which the bell was finally placed.

上京即事五首之二

萨都剌

祭天马酒洒平野,

沙际风来草亦香。

白马如云向西北,

紫驼银瓮赐诸王。

The Second Poem of Five
Regarding the Upper Capital

Sa Dula

they sprinkle the wine
fermented from the milk of horses
on the heaven worship day

wind blowing from the desert
carries the fragrance over the grassland

white horses race
like clouds scudding to the northwest

camels of pale reddish color
carry the wine in great silver jars

gifts from the emperor are given

to the delight of the nobles

The Upper Capital: After the Yuan Dynasty conquered the south of
China in 1279 Peking was chosen as the main capital but Kaiping which is
in the northeast of Duolun County in Inner-Mongolia of today was also set
up as the Upper Capital for use in summer.

上京即事五首之三

萨都剌

牛羊散漫落日下，

野草生香乳酪甜。

卷地朔风沙似雪，

家家行帐下毡帘。

The Third Poem of Five
Regarding the Upper Capital

Sa Dula

flocks of sheep and cattle
wander the low hills in sundown

the wild grass is fragrant
and the taste of the new cheese is good

the north wind comes in gales
whirling the sand like clouds of snow

families huddle in their tents

they secure the curtains
closing the entrances of their yurts

The Upper Capital: After the Yuan Dynasty conquered the south of China in 1279 Peking was chosen as the main capital but Kaiping which is in the northeast of Duolun County in Inner-Mongolia of today was also set up as the Upper Capital for use in summer.

宫 词

萨都剌

清夜宫车出建章,

紫衣小队两三行。

石栏干畔银灯过,

照见芙蓉叶上霜。

On Palace Life

Sa Dula

the world in deep silence and this night so late

the royal carriage rolls from the palace

followed by two or three lines of palace maids

dressed in their purple gowns

the silvery light from the lanterns they carry

gleams through the stone rails of the bridge

and makes the frost on the lotus leaves glow

燕姬曲

萨都剌

燕京女儿十六七，

颜如花红眼如漆。

兰香满路马尘飞，

翠袖短鞭娇欲滴。

春风澹荡摇春心，

锦筝银烛高堂深。

绣衾不暖锦鸳梦，

紫帘垂雾天沉沉。

芳年谁惜去如水，

春困着人倦梳洗。

夜来小雨润天街，

满院杨花飞不起。

A Pleasure Girl in the Capital

Sa Dula

she was just sixteen or seventeen
this one who could turn eyes in the capital

her face was the color of a pink rose
her eyes were the darkest lacquer

when she rode her pony through town
the dust whirled behind her
and a fragrance lingered in the wind

she would use her quirt
and you could see her silk sleeve

when she raised her small arm
the colors of the rainbow were flashing

the soft breezes in spring

set a thrill in her heart

the haunting sound of zithers

the gleam of candles in silver stands

but it was not embroidered bed spreads

that kept her warm from the cold

it was those who held her in her dreams

when she was shielded by curtains of purple silk

curtains hung in the doorways

mists of the night and dark skies were not for her

the passing away of youth

why make a lament for that

so much water over a dam

even in spring she does not hurry at all

she is too tired to get up in the mornings

and why should she bother with her hair

last night there was a drizzling rain
it wetted down the streets of the capital

the poplar blossom covered the yards
they could not fly into the air any more

别武昌

揭傒斯

欲归常恨迟，

将行反愁遽。

残年念骨肉，

久客多亲故。

伫立望江波，

江波正东注。

A Farewell to Wuchang

Jie Xisi

I wish I could return sooner to my hometown
I am distressed that I have delayed so long

but I feel sorry as well
as the moment for departure is almost here

my late years have gone to frost
and I have learned how an old man
misses the chatter of his relatives

but I have been a guest here so long
and I have made so many friends in this town
it will be painful saying goodbye to them

now I stand lost in silence
studying the waves on the river

and the current in this river

moving to the east with no hesitation

Wuchang is in Hubei Province on the Yangtze River. The poet's hometown Fengcheng is now in the east of Jiangxi Province.

夏五月武昌舟中触目

揭傒斯

两髯背立鸣双橹，

短蓑开合沧江雨。

青山如龙入云去，

白发何人并沙语。

船头放歌船尾和，

篷上雨鸣篷下坐，

推篷不省是何乡，

但见双飞白鸥过。

A Sight from Boating at Wuchang in Summer

Jie Xisi

the two old men have long beards
one stands in the bow
one in the stern

they face away from each other
splashing their oars in the river
making a pleasant music

their straw rain capes are short
opening and closing in the rain
as they bend over the water

there are green mountains
soaring into the clouds

they coil along the horizon
like so many dragons

who are the two white bearded fellows

talking with each other on the beach

the man in the bow sings his line

the stern sweep answers

now in the cabin

I sit awhile listening to the rain

when I push the wicker window open

I do not know where I am

I see two gulls wheeling overhead

Wuchang is in Hubei Province on the Yangtze River.

归 舟

揭傒斯

汀洲春草遍，

风雨独归时。

大舸中流下，

青山两岸移。

鸦啼木郎庙，

人祭水神祠。

破浪争掀舞，

艰难久自知。

Voyage Home

Jie Xisi

spring now and the islands
covered with a growth of tender grass

I am on my way back to the old homestead
making this long voyage in the rain by myself

the heavy vessel races in the current
mountains fall away on either side

crows make a commotion at the temple of the wood god
pilgrims bow in the shrine of the water god

now coming down this chute
the river batters our launch and the rigging groans

it is so much like my life
the hard conditions I knew long ago

墨 梅

王 冕

我家洗砚池头树，

朵朵花开淡墨痕。

不要人夸好颜色，

只留清气满乾坤。

Darkened Plum Blossoms

Wang Mian

the plum tree in my yard
grows alongside the little pond
where I wash my black ink-slab

all the blossoms are slightly darkened

not for them to seek compliments
for their lovely color

as they fill the air
with a fragrance that needs no color

The poet wrote about his own Chinese traditional black-white painting
of plum blossoms which is still well preserved in China.

西湖竹枝歌

杨维桢

石新妇下水连空，

飞来峰前山万重。

妾死甘为石新妇，

望郎或似飞来峰。

West Lake Bamboo Branch Song

Yang Weizhen

beneath the gaze of that woman called Shixinfu
who turned into stone after standing there too long
waiting for the return of her husband
there is nothing but water reflecting the clouds

beyond the Flying-over-Peak
which was said to have come from India
there are ranges over ranges

I would be willing to suffer death
turning myself into a stone woman
so that I could wait forever for my husband

I hope that he comes suddenly

like that Flying-over-Peak

that fell from the sky

Bamboo Branch was originally a folk song in Sichuan Province. Poet Liu Yuxi was the first one to start collecting, mimicking, and absorbing its essence in his own poem writing. **Shixinfu** is the name of a piece of rock standing beside West Lake in Hangzhou. It is also called Waiting-for-Husband Rock. This is from a legend that tells the story of a woman turning into this piece of rock after waiting for her husband to return home for a very long time. **Flying-over-Peak** is a peak on the Lingyin Mountain beside West Lake in Hangzhou. There is a legend about this name, which says this name is after a comment made one thousand six hundred years ago by a monk from India saying the peak was originally in India but flew over to Lingyin Mountain.

庐山瀑布谣

杨维桢

银河忽如瓠子决，

泻诸五老之峰前，

我疑天孙织素练，

素练脱轴垂青天。

便欲手把并州剪，

剪取一幅玻璃烟。

相逢云石子，

有似捉月仙。

酒喉无耐夜渴甚，

骑鲸吸海枯桑田。

居然化作十万丈，

玉虹倒挂清泠渊。

The Waterfall in Lu Mountain
Yang Weizhen

suddenly the milky way

crowds the heavens

like the yellow river

over flowing in the Huzi River

cascades rush down the Wulao Peak

I think maybe it is that

wonderful weaving fairy in the sky

shaking out her pure white spun silk fabric

it falls open in deep blue space

give me a pair of Bingzhou scissors

and I would cut out a panel

it would be all fog and smoke

but gleaming like a glass pane

I met Yunshizi on this spot

the poet was intelligent and romantic

much like Li Bai

a poet drowned in water for catching the moon

he upended a keg of wine

and he was still terribly thirsty that night

he went out and rode a whale

and drank the green sea dry

you can bet the floor of that ocean

will be prime bottom land for farmers

he then poured out what he drank

and that turned into a mile high waterfall

a crystalline rainbow of jade

rising from the deep and chilly pond

Lu Mountain is in Jiujiang, Jiangxi Province. The Huzi River is in Puyang County, He'nan Province where the Yellow River flooded in the Han Dynasty. Wulao Peak is the southern peak of Lu Mountain. Bingzhou scissors were scissors made in Bingzhou, a place along Taiyuan, Shanxi Province of today, well-known for its high quality scissors in ancient China. Yunshizi was Guan Yunshi, a popular poet in the Yuan Dynasty. Li Bai was a famous poet in the Tang Dynasty who was drowned while trying to catch the moon in a river from his boat after getting drunk according to legend.

北 里

倪 瓒

舍北舍南来往少，

自无人觅野夫家。

鸠鸣桑上还催种，

人语烟中始焙茶。

池水云笼茅草气，

井床露净碧桐花。

练衣挂石生幽梦，

睡起行吟到日斜。

North Village

Ni Zan

neighbours seldom visit one another here
no visitors come to my home

who would bother
looking for a recluse like me

turtle-doves are cooing in the mulberry trees
they want us to hurry with our plowing

I hear voices hidden in the mist
it is high time to cure the tea leaves

I can hardly see the pond
with all the grass and shrubs around it

beside the blossoming paulownia
the guard rail at the well shimmers with dew

I spread my coat on a boulder

and have a peaceful dream there

when I wake up

I walk along singing my poems

until the sun sets

京师得家书

袁 凯

江水三千里，

家书十五行。

行行无别语，

只道早还乡。

Here in the Capital
Receiving a Letter from Home

Yuan Kai

from hundreds of miles away

this letter from home finds me

oh it is a letter of many lines

I read it page by page

but what do I read there

come home soon

采莲歌

刘　基

女伴相随出芰荷，

并船比较采莲多。

抬头忽见游人过，

棹入菰蒲水拍坡。

A Song for Harvesting the Lotus Seeds

Liu Ji

these young women come together

their boats are drifting among

the water caltrops and the lotus blossoms

whenever two small boats meet

the women are so eager to know

who has gathered more lotus seeds

once the women see strangers passing by

they hurry among the reeds

and the tall stems of wild rice

only the waves they cause

ripple on the clay of the shoreline

五月十九日大雨

刘 基

风驱急雨洒高城，

云压轻雷殷地声。

雨过不知龙去处，

一池草色万蛙鸣。

Thunder Storm on the Nineteenth Day of the Fifth Month in the Lunar Calendar

Liu Ji

winds drove the fierce rain
beating against the gate tower
high above the city wall

massive clouds rolled their thunder
against the earth and shook it

where did that storm dragon vanish
when the rain stopped

now we have thousands of frogs
singing in the pond

and the pond is a perfect mirror
for the fresh grass after the storm

湖堤晓行

李　晔

宿云如墨绕湖堤，

黄柳青蒲咫尺迷。

行到画桥天忽醒，

谁家茅屋一声鸡。

Walking by the Lake at Dawn
Li Ye

the night sky is heavy with clouds

and dark as black ink

as I wander along the shore of the lake

yellow willow

and the green wands of cattail

blur just a few steps away

but when I walk up the painted bridge

suddenly the day rouses beneath the sun

and from a straw hut somewhere

a rooster struts out

闻邻船吹笛

杨 基

江空月寒露华白,

何人船头夜吹笛。

参差楚调转吴音,

定是江南远行客。

江南万里不归家,

笛里分明说鬓华。

已分折残堤上柳,

莫教吹落陇头花。

Hearing Someone Playing a Bamboo Flute on a Neighbouring Boat

Yang Ji

not a ripple on the surface of the water
the moon shedding a cold light
turns the dew to silver

who is that sitting on the bow of his boat
playing the bamboo flute at this late hour

I have heard such music in the center of the country
but then again there is something of the coast in it

this flute player must be a far traveler
south of the Yangtze River is a long way
more than thousands of miles I would guess

he cannot go back

and his hair is beginning to grey

I can tell from his music

so many have departed

the willows along the levee have been picked thin

poor gestures could not stop those friends

from saying goodbye

the flute player's music is so poignant

I hope it does not shake the plum blossoms

from their branches in the field

I need some to send home

Center of the country indicates the area of the Chu Kingdom (896 – 951), which is around today's Hu'nan Province. The coast indicates the area of the Wu Kingdom (222–280), which covers the southeast of China of today including the east coast. The willows along the levee have been picked thin reflects an old Chinese custom in which people broke branches off willows to express: "I'll miss you." when seeing someone off.

秋 望

高 启

霜后芙蓉落远洲，

雁行初过客登楼。

荒烟平楚苍茫处，

极目江南总是秋。

Looking at the Country in Autumn

Gao Qi

the lotus blossoms have fallen
the frost took them

they have drifted down stream
reaching a small island far and bare

when I ascended this tower
the geese were clamoring overhead

from here I can see
many trees on the horizon

and beyond that the land seems deserted
hidden in the blue haze of fall

and farther much farther away
I can see south of the Yangtze River
deep in fall of this year

明 朝 诗 选

The Ming Dynasty Poems

1368—1644

暮春遇雨

于 谦

暖风吹雨浥轻尘，

满地飞花断送春。

莫上高楼凝望眼，

天涯芳草正愁人。

Out in the Rain in Late Spring

Yu Qian

a warm wind brings the rain
and the rain settles the dust

and so brings the spring to an end
scattering petals everywhere in the garden

do not climb the steps up the pagoda
you will see a long way from there it is true
but only the green grass to the horizon

the memory of the lost spring flowers
will trouble your heart there

寄彭民望

李东阳

斫地哀歌兴未阑，

归来长铗尚须弹。

秋风布褐衣犹短，

夜雨江湖梦亦寒。

木叶下时惊岁晚，

人情阅尽见交难。

长安旅食淹留地，

惭愧先生苜蓿盘。

Writing to Peng Minwang

Li Dongyang

still at sixes and sevens

after humming your mournful tune

yes and stabbing the ground with your sword

you still need to knock on your scabbard

because no one knows your talent

you are living in your summer clothes

and the fall wind is sharp with cold

your tunic does not cover half your body

there is no warmth in those rough cottons

even your dreams are cold

they are cold with a cold fall rain

and you are wandering in some forgotten place

colder than the night you are dreaming in

it is shocking

the leaves are suddenly falling

the time is so late

the year is just about over

you know more downs than ups

and more troubles than I can count

well we all know how hard it is

when no friends come cheering your doorway

I can not abandon this place myself

I can still eke out a living

so I linger here wasting my time

what a way to live in the capital

really I feel so bad I can't help you

so ashamed of the clover in your plate

but I have almost nothing in my larder

I hold a position without power

Peng Minwang was a talented person from You County, Hu'nan Province. He lost favor from the emperor in his late years and retired. After he went back to his hometown he suffered from poverty.

闺 怨

周 在

江南二月试罗衣,

春尽燕山雪尚飞。

应是子规啼不到,

故乡虽好不思归。

Complaint of the Wife

Zhou Zai

it is in the second month of the moon
south of the Yangtze River
I should try on my spring clothes
they may be too loose for me

far in the north where my husband is
it must still be snowing on Yan Mountain

it is all the fault of the cuckoos
they can't be there in the north singing
good to go home good to go home

I don't think that my husband notices
how the seasons are changing

he is not even thinking of coming back

although I want to make it so good for him

Yan Mountain is in the north of Hebei Province, starting from Yang River and ending in the east of Shanhai Pass. Beijing is at the foot of Yan Mountain, along which is part of the Great Wall.

泛太湖

唐 寅

具区浩荡波无极,

万顷湖光尽凝碧。

青山点点望中微,

寒空倒浸连天白。

鸥夷一去经千年,

至今高韵人犹传。

吴越兴亡付流水,

空留月照洞庭船。

Boating on Tai Lake

Tang Yin

this lake does not seem to have a far shore

you see only waves beyond waves

horizons that are green mingled with light

green mountains distant and vague

drift here and there

with blue skies reflected in the crystal water

the noble Fan Li

has been gone for a thousand years

yet even to this day

the great man that he was is remembered

the rise and fall of Kingdoms Wu and Yue

they are so much water over the dam

nothing but water

only that same old moon

still shadows the boats on the lake

beside Dongting mountains

Tai Lake is in Wuxi, Jiangsu Province. Fan Li assisted the king of the Yue Kingdom in his conquest of the Wu Kingdom, but when Yue won the victory, Fan Li left secretly with his beautiful companion, the Lady Xi Shi, who was considered one of the four most beautiful women in ancient China. They drifted over Tai Lake in their boat, where no one would know who he was. Dongting mountains are the east and west Dongting mountains in the southeast of Tai Lake.

济上作

徐祯卿

两年为客逢秋节，

千里孤舟济水旁。

忽见黄花倍惆怅，

故园明日又重阳。

Poem Written on the Ji River

Xu Zhenqing

I have celebrated on my way
the Chongyang Festival twice

but this time my boat anchored alone
on the Ji River is a thousand
long miles from where I lived

and now I see the yellow flowers
these faithful chrysanthemums
and I am overcome with loneliness

tomorrow in my home village
it is the Chongyang Festival again

The Ji River is from Jiyuan County, He'nan Province, running into Shandong Province. Before running into the sea in the east it merged with the Yellow River. Chongyang Festival, a traditional holiday in China, is on the ninth day of the ninth month in the lunar calendar. On that day, family members climb hills together for sightseeing to welcome the season of fall.

在武昌作

徐祯卿

洞庭叶未下，

潇湘秋欲生。

高斋今夜雨，

独卧武昌城。

重以桑梓念，

凄其江汉情。

不知天外雁，

何事乐长征？

Poem Written in Wuchang

Xu Zhenqing

the leaves have not fallen yet

on Dongting Lake

but I can see the water is rising

in the Xiao and the Xiang rivers

it is a night full of rain

and I am alone resting in bed in Wuchang

I miss the mulberry and the catalpa trees

the good brace around my house

when I stare at the Yangtze and the Han River

I feel wretched

geese on the wild wing

they are so eager to leave the north

and I can't tell you why

Wuchang is in Hubei Province on the Yangtze River. The poet's hometown Fengcheng is now in the east of Jiangxi Province. The Dongting Lake
is in the North of Hu'nan Province, on the southern bank of the Yangtze
River. The Xiao and the Xiang rivers are both in Hu'nan Province. The Han
River runs into the Yangtze River at Wuchang.

答望之

何景明

念汝书难达，

登楼望欲迷。

天寒一雁至，

日暮万行啼。

饥馑饶群盗，

征求及寡妻。

江湖更摇落，

何处可安栖？

Answering Wangzhi

He Jingming

I have been missing you
but it is difficult to keep in touch with letters

I climb to the top of the pagoda now
and see nothing but a sad fall season

a single goose
labors into the cold air

it is sundown
and my eyes are wet with tears

there is so much suffering from calamity
gangs of thieves are everywhere

officials work overtime to collect taxes
they even go after the widows

the grass will dry out and the leaves will fall

where is a place that is safe and warm

Wangzhi was Meng Yang from Xinyang in He'nan Province, who wrote
a letter to the poet on his way to a new job in the south of the Yangtze River
while the poet was laid off due to political reasons.

柳

杨　慎

垂杨垂柳管芳年，

飞絮飞花媚远天。

金距斗鸡寒食后，

玉娥翻雪暖风前。

别离江上还河上，

抛掷桥边与路边。

游子魂销青塞月，

美人肠断翠楼烟。

Willows

Yang Shen

slender green shoots of the willows

they are the earliest tokens of spring

catkins float on the wind with a feminine charm

I think they are flirting with the skies

after Cold Food Day

there is cockfighting in the pits

the golden spurs flashing everywhere

butterflies flutter in the warm breezes

like snowflakes on a gentle day in winter

this is the time for departure by boat

branches broken off willows for remembrances

lie scattered on the roads and bridges

the ones who have gone to the borders

perhaps they feel lost there without spring

when they look at the cold moon

but the lonely women at home

see the willows tossing in the wind

like clouds of curling smoke

and the sad heart is their only friend

Cold Food Day is the day before Qingming Festival. It is a day for having only cold meals to avoid using fire in memory of a hero Jie Zitui who was burnt to death when the emperor ordered the mountain set on fire hoping to get this well-known hermit out so that the emperor could honor him. Qingming Festival is known for worshiping at the ancestral graves and sweeping graves for cleaning in spring. Branches broken off willows refer to an old Chinese custom which means "I'll miss you", when seeing someone off or saying goodbye to someone.

昆阳望海

杨　慎

昆明波涛南纪雄，

金碧滉漾银河通。

平吞万里象马国，

直下千尺蛟龙宫。

天外烟峦分点缀，

云中海树入空蒙。

乘槎破浪非吾事，

已斩鱼竿狎钓翁。

Looking at Kunming Lake from Kunyang

Yang Shen

the wildest waves in Kunming Lake
shatter the beach here in the south

the water races under the Milky Way
shimmering with flecks of gold

Kunming Lake is so broad
you cannot see the nations on the other side

those countries where armies
ride elephants and horses into battle

it is more than a thousand fathoms deep
you cannot reach the palace of the dragons

the mountain range along the shore
crests under lofty clouds in the sky

on the slopes of the hills beside the water

there are woods shrouded in mysteries of fog

serving the court is nothing I can do

as I am banished here like a prisoner

only long mornings with tackle box and my bait

I am one of the fishermen beside the lake

Kunming Lake is also called Tianchi in the southwest of Kunming, Yunnan Province. Kunyang is in Jinning, Yunnan Province.

怨歌行

谢 榛

长夜寒生翠幕低，

琵琶别调为谁凄？

君心无定如明月，

才照楼东复转西。

Song of Discontent

Xie Zhen

the night never ends
I have let down the curtains
but it is still cold

who are these sad notes for
the sound of the pipa strings
when I touch them one by one
the lord who loved me
he is changing like the moon

that was on the east side of my house
and now it drifts to the west side

Pipa is a four-stringed Chinese traditional plucked musical instrument
with a pear-shaped wooden body and a certain number of frets.

榆河晓发

谢 榛

朝晖开众山，

遥见居庸关。

云出三边外，

风生万马间。

征尘何日静，

古戍几人闲？

忽忆弃襦者，

空惭旅鬓斑。

Leaving at Dawn from the Yu River

Xie Zhen

when the dawn wakes the morning up
I can see the mountains
and Juyong Pass just visible in the distance

there are thunderclouds all along the border
thousands of horses gallop in the wind there

when will the dust of fighting settle
and the guards rest easy at their posts

suddenly I think of Han Zhongjun
throwing away his permit for return

I cannot match his ambition

my hair is already streaked with gray

Han Zhongjun gave up his pass when he entered Juyong Pass which is in the north of Beijing, as a selected student to study in the Capital. He was determined not to return home but to serve the emperor. Later he travelled through the Juyong Pass but armed with the emperor's commission.

和聂仪部明妃曲

李攀龙

天山雪后北风寒，

抱得琵琶马上弹。

曲罢不知青海月，

徘徊犹作汉宫看。

Rhymed as in Nie Yibu's poem — Ming Concubine

Li Panlong

after snow on the Tianshan Mountain
there was a bitter north wind

she rode a horse
plucking the four-string pipa

but after one song
she wondered where the moon was
above the barbaric land

it was the Han Palace

her thoughts were sad for

and the moon she saw there

Nie Yibu was Nie Jing, the poet's friend. His official title was Yibu. He was born in Yongfeng County, Jiangxi Province. **Ming Concubine** was a concubine of integrity who was never seen by Emperor Yuan in the Western Han Dynasty as she refused to bribe the court painter for a beautiful portrait of her as she was. The Emperor Yuan married her off to a barbarian king in the north for keeping peace. She did not hesitate since she thought she served the cause of her country. **Tianshan Mountain** is in Xinjiang Uygur Autonomous Region and Gansu Province. Its original name in the Huns' language was Qilian Mountain, which means sky mountain. In Chinese, sky is called tian and that's why it's called Tianshan. **Pipa** is a four-stringed Chinese traditional plucked musical instrument with a pear-shaped wooden body and a certain number of frets. **Han Palace** indicated the emperor's palace in the Han Dynasty.

登太白楼

王世贞

昔闻李供奉，

长啸独登楼。

此地一垂顾，

高名百代留。

白云海色曙，

明月天门秋。

欲觅重来者，

潺湲济水流。

On the Taibai Tower

Wang Shizhen

I have heard the story
how Li Bai ascended this tower alone
howling at the top of his lungs

and because he came here that one time
this place has been famous
for a hundred generations

at dawn the white clouds
gather to the sea
the autumnal moon
lingers in the clear heaven

you can look for another Li Bai now
but it is the Ji River

moving in its slow current

only the river that you will find

Taibai Tower is in Shandong Province. It got this name because the Rencheng County's governor, He Zhizhang, invited Li Bai (also known as Li Taibai), the famous poet, to have a drink there when the poet came to visit. The Ji River is from Jiyuan County, Henan Province, running into Shandong Province. Before running into the sea in the east it merged eventually with the Yellow River.

登盘山绝顶

戚继光

霜角一声草木哀，

云头对起石门开。

朔风边酒不成醉，

落叶归鸦无数来。

但使雕戈销杀气，

未妨白发老边才。

勒名峰上吾谁与？

故李将军舞剑台。

On the Top of Panshan Mountain

Qi Jiguang

the military bugle call
shatters the quiet on this cold morning
weeds underfoot have stiffened with frost

when the wind-drifted cloud passes over
I can see where the cliffs
open like a gate

standing on top of the mountain
I drink the wine fermented at this border
in this cold northern wind

it does not make me feel numb
no it rouses my fighting spirit

this is a world of fallen leaves
and crows beating against the wind

but if I can stop any invaders at this pass

what is it to me

even my hair will have turned grey

and the years will have bent my back

on the crest of the mountain

carved on the rock is Li Jing's victory story

I want my name to be bound up with this general

who danced with his sword here

Panshan Mountain is in the northwest of Ji County in Hebei Province. Its five peaks rise up above the ground, the highest one of which is Moon Hanging Peak. Qi Jiguang, the poet, was a famous general in the Ming Dynasty. General Li Jing was a highly respected general in the Tang Dynasty. The crest where general Li danced with his sword a thousand years ago has been known as Sword Dance Platform.

· 106 ·

酒店逢李大

徐　熥

偶向新丰市里过，

故人尊酒共悲歌。

十年别泪知多少，

不道相逢泪更多。

Happening to Meet Li Da in a Wine Shop

Xu Teng

one day passing through Xinfeng Town

I heard my old friend singing

he sang aloud but alone

the sad songs while drinking wine

oh we shed many a tear

during the decade we were apart

but how were we to know

there would be so many more

over our cups in the wine shop that day

Xinfeng Town: The site of this town is in the northeast of Lintong County, Shanxi Province, which was famous for wine drinking and became a symbol of wine shops. **Li Da** is possibly a nick name and there is no way to find any information about this man.

春日闲居

徐 熥

草阁春方暮，

柽阴日未斜。

蜗涎分断壁，

莺语共邻家。

曲坞藏修竹，

轻云覆落花。

卑栖有至性，

长此卧烟霞。

A Leisurely Life in Spring

Xu Teng

I live here in my straw hut
enjoying the late spring day

the tamarisk outside of my yard
spreads shade underneath to tell it is still noon

the snail has left its silver print
making a track down the broken wall

orioles are calling
in the gardens of my neighbourhood

the trail curves down the hill
groves of green bamboo alongside are visible

images of clouds dapple the hills
where fallen blossoms are scattered

I became aware in this place
how our lives grow at one with nature

this is the village I want to make my home
enjoying the beauty of the country

春 怨

谢肇淛

长信多春草，

愁中次第生。

君王行不到，

渐与玉阶平。

Sad Complaint in Spring

Xie Zhaozhe

Changxin Palace in early spring
the grass grows untended

sorrow rooted in my heart
grows deeper day by day

my lord never came here
the grass creeps over the stairs

Changxin Palace has long been used to symbolize that a concubine lost favor of the emperor. In the Western Han Dynasty (206 BC –25 AD), Emperor Cheng was in love with his new concubine Zhao Feiyan so that he put concubine Ban into Changxin Palace and refused to visit her. Thus Changxin Palace became a term to indicate a concubine who has been forgotten by the emperor.

郊外水亭小集

袁宏道

山自萧森涧自寒，

却怜胜地在长安。

桐荫恰好当窗覆，

柳色偏宜近水看。

已倦呼儿犹问酒，

不情逢客强加冠。

湘江亦有幽居处，

多少芙蓉忆钓竿。

Party at a Riverside Kiosk in the Suburb

Yuan Hongdao

the green trees are dense along the hills
cold air sweeps up from the deep ravine

this is a pleasant place
but what a pity it is not in the capital Chang'an

the parasol tree shades my windows
the lakeside willows are so attractive

I am so miserable in my heart
I ask my son to bring me more wine

garden parties like this one bore me
but I have to dress up for the occasion

I wish I could leave all this behind
live by myself on the bank of the Xiang River

as a recluse I could drop a solitary hook

my only companions would be lotus flowers

Chang'an was the capital of the Han Dynasty and the Tang Dynasty. Later it has been used to indicate capital. **Xiang River** is in Hu'nan Province running into Dongting Lake.

江行俳体

钟　惺

虚船也复戒偷关，

枉杀西风尽日湾。

舟卧梦归醒见水，

江行怨泊快看山。

弘羊半自儒生出，

馁虎空传税使还。

近道计臣心转细，

官钱曾未漏渔蛮。

Sailing on the Yangtze River

Zhong Xing

even with an empty boat

you have to wait for the tax collectors

and the wind rousing from the west

looks so good for an eastern sail

I slept in the boat during that day

and woke up where we were before

I stared again and again at the mountains

trying to control my anger

those in charge of the kingdom's finances

know nothing of real life but only books

like minister Sang Hongyang

tax collectors

those hungry tigers are ravenous
crouching to stalk the people

they have learned how to get more
with their new tax on fishermen
bleeding them dry in their boats

Sang Hongyang, minister of agriculture and in charge of finance in the
Han Dynasty, tried to encourage farming but repress trade.

瓶 梅

谭元春

入瓶过十日，

愁落幸开迟。

不借春风发，

全无夜雨欺。

香来清静里，

韵在寂寥时。

绝胜山中树，

游人或未知。

Plum Blossoms in a Vase

Tan Yuanchun

the plum branch in the vase
has been there for ten mornings
it started to bloom so late
but now I can still see the blossoms

the blossoms do not need
the soft encouragement of a spring breeze
and the bullying of the fierce night rain
holds no terror for them

theirs is a tranquil fragrance
something grown beautiful in isolation

how fine these are how much finer
than the plum tree shaken down in wilderness

there are of course those wanderers
who will not understand this

郊居杂兴

阮大铖

野绿何茫茫，

莫辨行人路。

我屋向山曲，

草树复纠互。

辟谷耻未能，

炊烟时一露。

遂引同心表，

琴书屏情愫。

恻睇城市间，

攘攘顿成误。

缘香蒲水壮，

清吹松风鹜。

于此话桑麻，

坐阅春山暮。

夷犹讵忍分，

茗糜聊已具。

Reflections on Living Far from the City

Ruan Dacheng

this is a rough land stretching so far

overgrown with weeds and bush

you cannot see where it ends

the pathways are obscured

my small house was built deep in the woods

it can hardly be seen

thick grass and the trees

form an impenetrable tangle

well I cannot do the fasting

the way prescribed and turn into a god

yes sometimes smoke from my cooking fire

wreathes the woods around my hut

people hereabouts are much the same

we share our thoughts in common

play the music and read books

enjoy the leisurely life

put aside the seductions of the mind

sometimes I think about life in the city

I feel sorry for those who cry after fame

following the fragrance to the wetlands

we see how the cattails grow strong

listening to the soft wind in the pines

when the ducks take flight

we chat with one another about farming

or what the harvest will bring

and sit there until the spring hills begin to darken

even then we are not ready to say goodbye

now with tea and a little porridge

we can go on talking half the night

田　家

黄淳耀

田泥深处马蹄奔，

县帖如雷过废村。

见说抽丁多不惧，

年荒已自鬻儿孙。

Farmer

Huang Chunyao

those agents from the local government
came spurring their horses
running wildly across the muddy fields

the notice from the governor
hit our empty village right after the flood
like another clap of thunder

but when the farmers knew
they came to force the young men to go with them
as volunteer laborers for the government
they were not afraid anymore

they didn't have anything to eat anyway
they were already selling their children for food

渡易水

陈子龙

并刀昨夜匣中鸣,

燕赵悲歌最不平。

易水潺湲云草碧,

可怜无处送荆卿。

Across the Yi River

Chen Zilong

the dagger honed in Bing County
rang in its scabbard last night

warriors from the Yan and Zhao Kingdoms
their hearts beat with songs of courage
and songs of sorrow

the water in the Yi River moves in quiet eddies
there are slender reeds along its banks

what a shame
what a shame

we cannot honor a Jing Ke again

who is also a brave warrior

setting out on his way

The **Yi River** rises from Yi County, in the west part of Hebei Province running into the Juma River. **Bing County** was famous for the high quality knife and scissors made there. **The Yan and Zhao Kingdoms** were two of the six Kingdoms all conquered by the Qin Kingdom. **Jing Ke**, trusted by Dan, the prince of the former Yan Kingdom, volunteered to attempt the assassination of the Emperor Qin Shihuang. This was to save the Yan Kingdom from the rule of the Qin Kingdom. Whether he succeeded or not, he would lose his life. The prince of the Yan Kingdom and Jing Ke's friends waved him farewell at the Yi River. They dressed themselves in the white garments of mourning.

小车行

陈子龙

小车班班黄尘晚，

夫为推，

妇为挽。

出门茫然何所之？

青青者榆疗我饥，

愿得乐土共哺糜。

风吹黄蒿，

望见垣堵，

中有主人当饲汝。

叩门无人室无釜，

踯躅空巷泪如雨。

The Wandering Wheelbarrow

Chen Zilong

the little barrow

drags a wheel through yellow dust

the axle squeaks and groans

late in the evening

the man pushes

and the woman in front

pulls it along

they don't know where they are going

so far from home

hoping to find a place to starve in

eating elm leaves

even in any place where

they can have a bowl of porridge

maybe very little grain in it

that would be paradise

the wind blowing over this land

beats down the withered stems of the sage

they see these broken walls

someone may be living in this place

people could be generous

and could feed them with some food

nobody answers

there is nothing in this house

not a dented pan

this lane is empty

their tears are as free as rain

There was a serious drought in north China in 1637. In Shandong Province there was a grasshopper plague. Harvest brought nothing, and hungry people all went elsewhere for food.

田园杂诗

钱澄之

春日不久晴，

衣垢及时浣。

身上何所著？

敝襦及骭短。

家人念我寒，

一杯为斟满。

酒满不可多，

农事不可缓。

奋身田野间，

襟带忽以散。

乃知四体勤，

无衣亦自暖。

君看狐貉温，

转使腰肢懒。

Poem Written in the Country

Qian Chengzhi

good weather does not last long in spring

we wash our soiled clothes as we can

when the days are clear

we put only the old clothes on our backs

the unlined long gown reaches hardly below the knees

my wife thinks I am cold

she pours me a brimful of liquor

I can only drink so much

farming in spring cannot be delayed

working up a sweat in the fields

I have to loosen my clothes

when you work with your hands

you don't need clothes to keep warm

take a look at those people

who walk around in fox-fur coats

they don't work and their bodies turn soft

即　事

夏完淳

战苦难酬国，

仇深敢忆家！

一身存汉腊，

满目尽胡沙。

落月翻旗影，

清霜冷剑花。

六军浑散尽，

半夜起悲笳。

Painful Thoughts

Xia Wanchun

I have been through the bitter fighting

but there is no saving this country

I had such hatred

such a desire for vengeance

I did not care about myself

my own protection

I will always call this my country

even though the northern invaders

have made it their own

the light of the setting moon

floods the banners of my army

we can see their wavering shadows

it is a cold pure frost

that paints our cold swords

the army rose up here once
against the enemy army
now they are all gone

the northern reed pipes
playing at midnight
there is so much sorrow in those songs

The northern invaders in this poem were soldiers from the Qing Kingdom, who captured the north of the Ming Dynasty and now the south. The
poem was written at the end of the Ming Dynasty in 1646.

清 朝 诗 选

The Qing Dynasty Poems

1616—1911

和盛集陶落叶 (之二)

钱谦益

秋老钟山万木稀，

凋伤总属劫尘飞。

不知玉露凉风急，

只道金陵王气非。

倚月素娥徒有树，

履霜青女正无衣。

华林惨淡如沙漠，

万里寒空一雁归。

Reply to "**Fallen Leaves**" *by Sheng Jitao in the Same Rhyme Sequence* (*No. 2*)

Qian Qianyi

the trees are bare on Zhong Mountain

the leaves are ashes in late fall

it was a surprise that cold wind coming

the dew was frozen white in the empty fields

but it will be no surprise

when the spirit of kingdom in Jinling vanishes

the lonesome goddess Chang'e in the moon

her companion is only a laurel tree

the goddess of frost and snow Qingnü

hardly has any clothes to wear

the woods once graceful are withered now

a single goose turns south in the cold sky

Sheng Jitao was Sheng Sitang, a poet from Tongcheng, Anhui Province, who lived in Nanjing, Jiangsu Province in the early years of the Qing Dynasty. Zhong Mountain is also called Zijin Mountain in the east of Nanjing. Jinling was the other name of Nanjing. Chang'e was a daughter of one of the earliest emperors before 3000 BC in Chinese legend, who secretly took the medicine her husband got from the heavens and flew all of a sudden into the moon and was supposed to stay there forever. Qingnü is the goddess in Chinese mythology, who is in charge of frost and snow.

追　悼

吴伟业

秋风萧索响空帏，

酒醒更残泪满衣。

辛苦共尝偏早去，

乱离知否得同归。

君亲有愧吾还在，

生死无端事总非。

最是伤心看稚女，

一窗灯火照鸣机。

Mourning

Wu Weiye

the wind is so cold this fall
ruffling the curtains of my empty bed

I wake from a drunken sleep late at night
and find my tears have soaked my clothes

she was taken from me so suddenly
after all the hardship we shared

now I don't know whether I will be buried with her
nothing is predictable with war and all

I am loyal to my late emperor and parents
now I am ashamed to live on in this world

everything has gone wrong
death and existence wife and dynasty

it is the most painful seeing my little daughter

and her mother's loom in the light at the window

又酬傅处士山次韵 （之一）

顾炎武

清切频吹越石笳，

穷愁犹驾阮生车。

时当汉腊遗臣祭，

义激韩雠旧相家。

陵阙生哀回夕照，

河山垂泪发春花。

相将便是天涯侣，

不用虚乘犯斗槎。

Reply to Fu Shan's Poem with the Same Rhyme (No. 1)

Gu Yanwu

you render sorrowful music
on the nomad reed flute like Yueshi

you are poor and overcome with worry
go out in your horse drawn cart like Ruan Ji

Chen Xian was loyal to the old Han Dynasty
he used the old Han ceremony when he offered sacrifice

Zhang Liang from the family of premier of the Han Kingdom
spent the family treasure to hire an assassin

it is heartbreaking in the sunset
seeing the palace and the tomb of the late emperor

even the rivers and mountains shed tears

but this at least will bring flowers in the spring

it is good for us old colleagues to keep company

as if we were going a long way together

we do not need to raft on the sea

carrying us to the star altar in the heavens

Fu Shan (1607–1683) was from Yangqu, Shanxi Province, became a recluse wearing Taoist gown and refused to work for the government of the Qin Dynasty after the Ming Dynasty was conquered and overthrown. **Yueshi** was Liu Kun, who lived in Taiyuan, Shanxi Province in the Jin Dynasty. When his town was surrounded by Hu soldiers, his playing of the nomad reed flute made enemy soldiers cry and leave. **Ruan Ji** refused to cooperate with the king of the Wei Kingdom in the Three Kingdoms period. When the king got the power after a palace coup he ran around in his cart aimlessly and wept after the horse found nowhere to go. **Chen Xian** resigned from his government position after the coup in the Han Dynasty (206 BC–25 AD) staged by Wang Mang. He said his ancestors never heard of the new kingdom so that he used the old Han Dynasty's memorial ceremony. **Zhang Liang** attempted to revenge the Qin Kingdom against the First Emperor of Qin because the Han Kingdom, his home country, was conquered by the Qin Kingdom, the king of which was the First Emperor of Qin.

钱塘观潮

施闰章

海色雨中开，

涛飞江上台。

声驱千骑疾，

气卷万山来。

绝岸愁倾覆，

轻舟故溯洄。

鸱夷有遗恨，

终古使人哀。

Watching the Tide at the Qiantang River

Shi Runzhang

there it is in the distance
the gray sea sullen under rain

and here the powerful waves rolling in
almost crash our lookout

the roaring of the tide from the ocean
this is like hundreds of stampeding horses

the air whirls with thousands of mountains
the cliff's face seems afraid it will collapse

beneath us a single launch
the boat heads for the coming waves

this is where they dropped the water bag
inside was the dead body of that premier

now his wrath will never be washed away

and people come to feel it and feel sad forever

The Qiantang River is in Zhejiang Province. The rising tide from the sea rushed into the mouth of the Qiantang River pushing the river's current back to create huge waves. The dead body of that premier refers to the story of Wu Zixu, the premier of the Wu Kingdom , who was forced to commit suicide by the king because the king believed in the words of a spy sent by the Yue Kingdom, the rival of the Wu Kingdom. The king of the Wu Kingdom ordered soldiers to put Wu Zixu's dead body into a water bag and to drop it into the Qiantang River. Later in the legend, the premier became god of the tide.

舟中立秋

施闰章

垂老畏闻秋，

年光逐水流。

阴云沉岸草，

急雨乱滩舟。

时事诗书拙，

军储岭海愁。

泮饥今有岁，

倚棹望西畴。

Boating on the Day Autumn Begins

Shi Runzhang

it is frightening to know
the coming of autumn when getting old

time is like a torrent
rushing over rocks in mountains

dark clouds make shadows in the grass
here on the river bank

the fishing boats are secured at the beach
they toss in the wind and rain

poems and books have always absorbed me
I am not a good man at a party

south of the five hills in Guangdong
the preparations for war never end

and hunger has squatted in many places

all these sad years

I can only look at the fields from the boat

bare plots stretching away to the west

Guangdong is a province in the south of China.

白桃花次乾斋侍读韵

王丹林

相逢不信武陵村，

合是孤峰旧托根。

流水有情空蘸影，

春风无色最销魂。

开当玉洞谁知路？

吹落银墙不见痕。

多恐赚他双舞燕，

误猜梨院绕重门。

Reply in the Same Rhyme Sequence to "White Peach Blossoms" by Qianzhai Who Is the Teacher of the Emperor

Wang Danlin

when I saw the white peach blossoms
I knew they were not from Wuling Village

these blossoms were so pale
I would have thought they were grafted
from the roots of the plums on Gu Peak

the river is like an unhappy lover
left with only the shadows of the blossoms
reflected in its running water

the spring wind has no color at all
but that wind must have magic tenderness
people get overwhelmed in it

when they bloom at the entrance of that village

everyone mistakes the road home

as they come blinking into pure white

the petals float in the wind here

when they stick to the white washed walls

who can tell where they have gone

look now how even the swallows

darting and circling mate with mate near the doors

seem to be confused

they cannot distinguish these blossoms

from the etched ivory of pear trees in spring

Qianzhai was Chen Yuanlong, from Haining, Zhejiang Province. Wuling
Village is a place depicted in Peach Blossom Paradise by Tao Yuanming, a
very popular poet in the Jin and Song Dynasties, which is located at
Changde area in Hu'nan Province. Gu Peak is by West Lake in Hangzhou,
Zhejiang Province.

船中曲 (之四)

吴嘉纪

侬是船中生，

郎是船中长。

同心苦亦甘，

弄篙复荡桨。

Boatman Songs *(No. 4)*

Wu Jiaji

I was born in a boat
my husband grew up in a boat

we have a hard life
but we are not bitter

we care about each other
and we have a sweet time

we are very good with a boathook
and we know how to handle the oars

云中至日

朱彝尊

去岁山川缙云岭，

今年雨雪白登台。

可怜至日长为客，

何意天涯数举杯？

城晚角声通雁塞，

关寒马色上龙堆。

故园望断江村里，

愁说梅花细细开。

On the Winter Solstice in Yunzhong

Zhu Yizun

at Jinyun Mountain this time last year
and at the lookout on Baideng Mountain
this year with rain and snow

it is miserable to be on the road again
on the winter solstice in Yunzhong

this is so far away from my family
I don't know why so frequently
I raise my wine cup alone

the military bugles sound on the border
you hear them at night even at Yanmen Pass

they stamp into the desert outside the Great Wall
herds of horses seem forlorn in the cold wind

I look to the south for my river village
but my home is far beyond the horizon

the plum blossoms opening slowly there
it is painful remembering

Yunzhong is Datong in Shanxi Province today. Jinyun Mountain is in Jinyun County, Zhejiang Province. Baideng Mountain is in Datong. Yanmen Pass is in the northwest of Dai County, Shanxi Province.

酬洪昇

朱彝尊

金台酒坐擘红笺，

云散星离又十年。

海内诗家洪玉父，

禁中乐府柳屯田。

梧桐夜雨词凄绝，

薏苡明珠谤偶然。

白发相逢岂容易，

津头且缆下河船。

Responding to Hong Sheng

Zhu Yizun

once we drank together at the Gold Stage
we wrote replies each other's poems

now ten years have gone
the clouds disbursed and the stars scattered

you reminded me that splendid poet Hong Yufu
and Liu Tuntian, master of song lyrics in the palace

the opera *Hall of Long Life* brought you fame
those beautiful and sorrowful lines you wrote

but like how scandal victimized a man
the seeds from plant job's tears could be pearls

well old friend your hair is as grey as mine
it will not be easy for us to meet again

so let me anchor my boat in the harbor

the night is for our old times

Hong Sheng wrote an opera titled *Hall of Long Life* (1688), but he was removed from office because he had his opera rehearsed in his home while the whole country was in mourning for the emperor's mother (1689). Gold Stage was built by the king of the Yan Kingdom in the Warring States period for attracting talented people to work for the king. The site of it is in the southeast of Yi County, Hebei Province. This gathering mentioned in the poem happened in Beijing. Hong Yufu (Hong Yan) and Liu Tuntian (Liu Yong) were both popular poets in the Song Dynasty. A man mentioned in the poem refers to Ma Yuan, an official in the Han Dynasty (206 BC–220 AD), who was reported to transport a load of pearls to his hometown from his post in Jiaozhi, but in fact that was a load of seeds from plant job's tears.

读陈胜传

屈大均

闾左称雄日，

渔阳谪戍人。

王侯宁有种？

竿木足亡秦。

大义呼豪杰，

先声仗鬼神。

驱除功第一，

汉将可谁伦？

After Reading the Biography of Chen Sheng

Qu Dajun

he was no more than a poor man
conscripted to guard the Yuyang border

why should an emperor be born to be an emperor
a revolt will bring the Qin Kingdom down

he borrowed the names of earlier heroes
set himself up with the people that way

and he called on the gods and spirits
and how could the people not believe in him

but death cut him short of a victory and even so
he was the one who shattered the Qin Dynasty

who then was the equal to this brave man

not all the generals from the Han Dynasty

Chen Sheng (?–208 BC) rose from a poor man and an ordinary soldier to become the leader of the rebellion against the Qin Dynasty in 209 BC and won great victories but finally was killed in a battle. However, his rebellion paved the way for the success of the Han Dynasty established in 206 BC. Yuyang was an ancient county's name. Its site is in the southwest of Miyun County, Hebei Province.

壬戌清明作

屈大均

朝作轻云暮作阴，

愁中不觉已春深。

落花有泪因风雨，

啼鸟无情自古今。

故国江山徒梦寐，

中华人物又消沉。

龙蛇四海归无所，

寒食年年怆客心。

Qingming Festival in 1682

Qu Dajun

thin layers of clouds in the morning

darken as evening comes

in my sadness I do not notice

it has been so late in spring

the battered blossoms

weep over in wind and rain

since when it has been known

birds full of song chirp heartlessly

and this land of my old dynasty

it is a lost country that haunts my dreams

those heroes have been depressed

they are all gone and who knows where

there are still many like dragons in the sea

they have no one to follow

each year on Cold Food Day

as a traveler my heart sinks under a stone

Qingming Festival is known for memorial services, worshipping at the ancestral graves and sweeping graves clean. Cold Food Day is the day before Qingming Festival. It is a festival for having cold meals only to avoid using fire in memory of a hero — Jie Zitui who was burned to death when the emperor ordered the mountain set on fire hoping to get this well-known hermit out so that he could honor him because Jie Zitui once saved the emperor's life.

题西洋画 (之一)

陈恭尹

西番画法异常伦，

如雾如烟总未真。

酷似少翁娱汉武，

隔帏相望李夫人。

Commentary on a Western Painting (*No. 1*)

Chen Gongyin

the way of painting in the west is peculiar

as if images are behind much fog or smoke

it seems to me as the image of concubine Li

Shaoweng conjured up for Emperor Wu in the Han Dynasty

he could only see her through many curtains

her image shadowed in candle light

Shaoweng was a necromancer in the Han Dynasty who tried to enter-
tain Emperor Wu as the emperor was longing so much for his favorite concubine Li who passed away.

南将军庙行

王士祯

范阳战鼓如轰雷，

东都已破潼关开。

山东大半为贼守，

常山平原安在哉！

睢阳独遏江淮势，

义激诸军动天地。

时危战苦阵云深，

裂眦不见官军至。

谁欤健者南将军，

包胥一哭通风云。

抽矢誓仇气慷慨，

拔剑堕指何嶙峋。

贺兰未灭将军死，

呜呼南八真男子。

中丞侍郎同日亡，

碧血斓斑照青史。

淮山峨峨淮水深，

庙门遥对青枫林；

行人下马拜秋色，

一曲淋铃万古心。

At the Shrine of General Nan

Wang Shizhen

the battle drums boomed in Fanyang

the rebel forces broke into the eastern capital

then they overran Tong Pass

they pillaged Changshan and Pingyuan

and they ravaged

everything in the east of the Hua Mountain

only the pass at Zhuiyang was secure

a barrier to the south of the Yangtze River

soldiers fought with furious courage

their shrieks of death shocked the heavens

and set the earth trembling

but there was no sign of relief troops

general Nan broke through the rebel lines

looking for help from the southern forces

but the warlord Helan refused him

his bravery was like Shen Baoxu in history

who went to Qin asking for help

he cried for seven days and seven nights

general Nan shot an arrow into the watch tower

a signal that he would return for vengeance

and he cut his own finger off

showing he would never league with such a man

but it was not to be

the general returned to the fight and captured

he was executed when he refused to surrender

oh what a man of courage he was

commander Zhang Xun and his assistant Yao Yan

were assassinated on the same day

defiant even after the city fell

their blood shines in the history of this land

the Huai River is running deep

and the mountains along it are rising high

there is a maple grove

opposite the entrance to the shrine of the general

travelers dismount their horses

and bow to show their respect for the fall colors

I am writing this sad poem for the past

like the *Bell in the Rain* the Tang's emperor wrote

General Nan was Nan Jiyun, from Dunqiu, the site of which is in the southwest of Qingfeng, Hebei Province. He fought till the very end and was captured and killed for refusing to surrender. **The Shrine of General Nan** was built in Si County, Anhui Province. **Fanyang** was an old name of a county, the site of which is in Jixian, in the southwest of Beijing. The An Lushan rebellion started from here in 755. **The Eastern Capital** was Luoyang, in He'nan Province. **Tong Pass** is in Tongguan County, Shanxi Province. **Changshan** is in Ding County, Hebei Province. **Zhang Xun** and **Yao Yan** were both high-ranking officials of the Tang Dynasty and were both persecuted because they refused to surrender. **Huai River** starts from Tongbai Mountain in Tongbai County, Nanyang City, He'nan Province running through He'nan, Anhui and Jiangsu provinces. *Bell in the Rain* was written by the Tang Emperor Xuanzong in 757 while fleeing to Sichuan Province but being caught in a non-stop rain.

秋柳 (之一)

王士祯

秋来何处最销魂？

残照西风白下门。

他日差池春燕影，

只今憔悴晚烟痕。

愁生陌上黄骢曲，

梦远江南乌夜村。

莫听临风三弄笛，

玉关哀怨总难论。

Willows in Fall (No. 1)

Wang Shizhen

where is the most exhilarating place
I can visit in the fall

the white gate to the city of Nanjing
where it catches the rays of the sundown

back and forth or high and low the wings
draw images of swallows in springtime

but given a fall evening
smoke from the cooking fires drifts there

someone is singing in the fields
the song of the war horse Huangcong

and now my dream
drifts towards the south of the Yangtze River

one night an empress was born there

and what a ruckus the crows made in Wuye Village

do not listen to the sound of the flute

that always drifts here with the wind

the grief it carries from Yumen Pass

still hurts too much to think of it

Nanjing is now the capital of Jiangsu Province. **Huangcong** was the Tang Dynasty emperor Tangtaizong's favorite steed that died on the way to war in the northeast. **Wuye Village** was the birthplace of Emperor Mu's wife in the Jin Dynasty (317–420). **The Yangtze River** is Changjiang. **Yumen Pass** is in the southwest of Dunhuang, Gansu Province.

真州绝句（之四）

王士禛

江干多是钓人居，

柳陌菱塘一带疏。

好是日斜风定后，

半江红树卖鲈鱼。

Jueju — a Four-line Poem
with Seven Words to a Line: Zhenzhou (No. 4)

Wang Shizhen

most people who live by the river are fishermen
their cottages are scattered along the bank

there are water-nuts or lotus in some ponds
visible along a field path lined with willows

it is sunset on the river
and the wind calms down with the fading light

and a good half of the river
gleams with the red reflections of sunlit trees

some fishermen on the bank have set up their stalls
they are selling the day's catch of perch

Zhenzhou is now in the Yizheng County in Jiangsu Province. It's on the northern shore of the Yangtze River.

过许州

沈德潜

到处陂塘决决流，

垂杨百里罨平畴。

行人便觉须眉绿，

一路蝉声过许州。

Traveling Through Xuzhou

Shen Deqian

everywhere here there are ponds
and the sound of running water

the level fields beneath the willows
stretch for a hundred miles

travelers think beards and eyebrows
are sprouting leaves

I make my journey through Xuzhou
with the drone of cicadas all around me

Xuzhou is now in Xuchang city, He'nan Province.

江 村

沈德潜

苦雾寒烟一望昏，

秋风秋雨满江村。

波浮衰草遥知岸，

船过疏林竟入门。

俭岁四邻无好语，

愁人独夜有惊魂。

子桑卧病经旬久，

裹饭谁令古道存？

The River Village

Shen Deqian

a bitter fog and cold smoke
the village looks miserable in the dimlight

the fall wind and rains
envelop the village in the evening

I know we are close to the river bank
rotted weeds are trailing in the waves

and my boat enters the yard of my friend
after sailing through a scattering of trees

this is such a lean year
I do not see in the neighbourhood a smiling face

my friend is sick and alone tonight
he is surprised when I knock on his door

he is not so lucky as Zi Sang in the old story

who was ill for ten rain-swept days

but a friend came with cooked rice to see him

it is not the same in these harsh hours

Zi Sang was from a story in a classical book *Zhuangzi*. Once it rained for ten days and his friend Zi Yu came to see him with some cooked food.

秋宿葛岭涵青精舍（之二）

厉 鹗

书灯佛火影清凉，

夜半层楼看海光。

蕉飔暗廓虫吊月，

无人知是半闲堂。

Staying for a Night in the Hanqing Temple on Ge Ridge in the Fall (No. 2)

Li E

I can read beside the candles
flickering in the eyes of the buddha

the walls are deep in cold shadows
and the glow of the burning joss sticks

at midnight I climb up to the top of the temple
and wish I could find some light from the sea

Chinese banana leaves tremble alongside the temple
insects make their sad songs for the moon

as if they know when
the full moon will become a crescent

no one seems to know at this time

the mansion was once Half Leisure Hall

The mansion on Ge Ridge in Hangzhou built by Jia Sidao who was premier of the Song Dynasty with the emperor's permission for worshipping Buddha, was called Half Leisure Hall.

晓登韬光绝顶

厉 鹗

入山已三日，

登顿遂真赏。

霜磴滑难践，

阳崖曦乍晃。

穿漏深竹光，

冷翠引孤往。

冥搜灭众闻，

百泉同一响。

蔽谷境尽幽，

跻颠瞩始爽。

小阁俯江湖，

目极但莽苍。

坐深香出院，

青霭落池上。

永怀白侍郎，

愿言脱尘鞅。

Climbing at Dawn to the Top of the Mountain Where Taoguang Temple Stands

Li E

three days in the mountains
it was exhilarating on the high ranges

frost covers this stone stairway
and it is chancy underfoot

those cliffs facing east
they are gleaming with morning light

but in the bamboo groves
just a dapple of sunshine falls here and there

alone I follow the green cold into the woods
where the sounds of the world are shut out

and all about me the springs

flow from the earth with the same music

it is so peaceful
such serenity in that shadowy valley

when I am on the top of the high mountain
the wide world below looks so different

this kiosk towers above the river and the lake
and I can look into the distance

and it is a breathtaking world I see
a nature I am powerless to penetrate

now as I linger in the small court of the temple
I breathe in the fragrance of incense

and far off as the sun rises
the mists from the hills settle on the pool

I will always remember Bai Juyi
who exchanged poems with monk Taoguang

I wish that I could put my world behind me

and live as a free man

Taoguang Temple is on the south hill of the mountain, in the north of West Lake in Hangzhou, where Monk Taoguang in the Tang Dynasty resided. Bai Juyi was a famous poet in the Tang Dynasty.

杭州半山看桃花

马曰璐

山光焰焰映明霞，

燕子低飞掠酒家。

红影到溪流不去，

始知春水恋桃花。

Peach Blossoms on Ban Hill in Hangzhou

Ma Yuelu

red blossoms of the peach trees on the hill

their burning flames color the clouds

swallows skim the roofs of the wine shops

the current in the river flows on

but the image of the blossoms remains

then I know the spring stream

falls in love with the blossoms

Ban Hill is outside of the Gen Gate, in the northeast suburbs of Hangzhou.

马嵬 (之二)

袁 枚

莫唱当年《长恨歌》，

人间亦自有银河。

石壕村里夫妻别，

泪比长生殿上多。

At the Wayside Station in Mawei (No. 2)

Yuan Mei

don't just sing that *Forever Regret Song*
the emperor and his concubine Yang

separated in this life on earth
just as in the folktale the Milky Way

an old man was forced into battle there
he bid farewell to his wife in Shihao Village

tears were more bitter with loss

than those in the Hall of Long Life

Mawei: The Tang Dynasty emperor Tangxuanzong escaped to Sichuan when An Lushan Rebellion took place. On his way at Mawei he had his beloved concubine strangled because of the pressure from his followers who believed this woman had corrupted the emperor. *Forever Regret Song* is a poem about the above tragic story written by Bai Juyi. **In the folktale the Milky Way** refers to the old legend in which the cowherd **(Altair)** married the fairy maiden from the heavens **(Vega),** but after giving birth to two children, the fairy maiden was taken away by her parents — King and Queen of the heavens. With the help of a piece of skin offered by a cow, he flew up to the sky with their two children to chase after her but he couldn't cross over the Milky Way. As a result, they were allowed to meet once a year on the evening on the seventh day of the seventh month in the lunar calendar. Since then magpies gather on top of the Milky Way to form a bridge with their wings to help with the reunion in that evening. **Shihao Village** was from Du Fu's Poem *Shihao Officials*. **The Hall of Long Life** was in Huaqing Palace, where the emperor Tangxuanzong and his concubine Yang swore to each other to be together forever.

遣兴 (之二)

袁 枚

但肯寻诗便有诗，

灵犀一点是吾师。

夕阳芳草寻常物，

解用多为绝妙词。

A Brief Insight *(No. 2)*

Yuan Mei

if I want to find it
the poem will be there

my mind always follows the inspiration
and my heart beats for it in unison

like the thread and core in a rhinoceros horn
it is thin but connecting the two ends

sunset and wind ruffled grass
these are common enough

but if I know and feel them deep down
everything can be a wonder in poems

富春至严陵山水甚佳

纪　昀

浓似春云淡似烟，

参差绿到大江边。

斜阳流水推篷坐，

翠色随人欲上船。

Enjoying the Landscape While Sailing from Fuchun to Yanling Mountain

Ji Yun

like clouds in spring their dark turmoil

or the smoke of cooking fires pale and vanishing

so many shades of green in these mountains

growing all the way down to the riverside

the sunset gleaming on the water

fills my small boat with light

then the shadows of this green world crowd me

taking over green on green aboard my boat

Fuchun is now Fuyang County. **Yanling Mountain** is in Tonglu County. Fuchun and Yanling Mountain are both in Zhejiang Province.

南池杜少陵祠堂

蒋士铨

先生不仅是诗人，

薄宦沉沦稷契身。

独向乱离忧社稷，

直将歌哭老风尘。

诸侯宾客犹相忌，

信史文章自有真。

一饭何曾忘君父，

可怜儒士作忠臣。

The Memorial Temple for Du Fu in Nanchi

Jiang Shiquan

you were not only the poet

you were as noble as Ji and Qi

ministers popular in the Shun Era

offices of lesser officials

these were not for you

you were never able to hold on to them

you with all your sad songs

and your worry about the kingdom and people

you were a splinter in the thumb of the kingdom

and you grew into your old years

knowing the long highways

the roads of the miserable traveler

but even an offer of high rank

could not detain you

you wrote about what was real in this life
you understood the sorrow of the people

and still you never forgot the emperor
you saluted him at every meal

you were to the end
the thoughtful official
the true disciple of Confucius

Du fu was one of the greatest poets in the Tang Dynasty. **Nanchi** is in Sichuan Province. **Shun Era** was around 2300 BC. **Confucius** (551 BC–479 BC) was from the Lu Kingdom during the Spring and Autumn Period. His name was Kong Qiu. He was the founder of Confucianism and is considered as a thinker and an educator in Chinese history.

题王石谷画册

蒋士铨

不写晴山写雨山,

似呵明镜照烟鬟。

人间万象模糊好,

风马云车便往还。

A Poem on the Collection of Paintings by Wang Shigu

Jiang Shiquan

the mountain you paint is in rain

never in sunshine

the green hills look like coiled hair of a woman

seen in a mirror breathed on

make the world as mysterious as you can

think how much better that is

I found in them high winds like horses

and clouds as chariots going back and forth

Wang Shigu was Wang Hui (1632 –1717) from Changshou, Jiangsu Province. He was a very successful artist, one of the four best artists at his time, painting in the early years of the Qing Dynasty.

西湖晤袁子才喜赠

赵 翼

不曾识面早相知，

良会真成意外奇。

才可必传能有几？

老犹得见未嫌迟。

苏堤二月春如水，

杜牧三生鬓有丝。

一个西湖一才子，

此来端不枉游资。

To Yuan Zicai after Meeting Him at West Lake

Zhao Yi

I knew about you long before
this occasion is so extraordinary

it is a rare chance to find a man of your talent
it is a miracle that I meet you when I am so old

it is spring time on Su Causeway
the world is as the water in the lake

perhaps the poet Du Mu was reborn
with all his talents in you and your grey hair

now to see west lake and to meet such a poet

my visit here was worth the gold it costs

Yuan Zicai (Yuan Mei) and the author were both famous poets in the south of the Yangtze River in the Qing Dynasty. They met at West Lake in 1779. The Su Causeway as named after a famous poet Su Shi in the Song Dynasty, who finished this project when he was the governor of Hangzhou in 1089. Du Mu was a very popular poet in the Tang Dynasty.

后园居诗

赵 翼

有客忽叩门，

来送润笔需。

乞我作墓志，

要我工为谀。

言政必龚黄，

言学必程朱。

吾聊以为戏，

如其意所须。

补缀成一篇，

居然君子徒。

核诸其素行，

十钧无一铢。

其文倘传后,

谁复知贤愚?

或且引为据,

竟入史册摹。

乃知青史上,

大半亦属诬。

One of the Poems Written While Living in a Back Garden

Zhao Yi

suddenly there is a knock at the door

someone brings me a stipend

he wants an epitaph

some memorable and kind words

he wants me to record

his official deeds and these

as noteworthy as those of Gong Sui and Huang Ba

and he wants me to commend

his knowledge and learning

comparing him to Cheng Hao, Cheng Yi and Zhu Xi

well I do it just for fun

but I try to satisfy the man's desire

after I put this and that together to finish

I am surprised that the man ended up a decent man

but thinking of his behavior in daily life

the difference is between a thousand and a ten

who can tell if the man was good or bad years later

or someone quotes my words as evidence

that might be sucked into the history books

so we know in those pages of our histories

most of them rubberneck the truth

Gong Sui and Huang Ba were high-ranking officials in the Han Dynasty considered by people as admirable officials in history. **Cheng Hao and Zhu Xi** were well-known Neo-Confucianism philosophers in the Song Dynasty.

论 诗

赵 翼

李杜诗篇万口传，

至今已觉不新鲜。

江山代有才人出，

各领风骚数百年。

On Poetry

Zhao Yi

Li Bai and Du Fu
oh generations honored their poems

but times change and tastes also
their poems are out of date now

fresh talent appears from time to time
new poets usher in new poetries

each should also be honored
for centuries to come

Li Bai and Du fu were among the greatest poets in the Tang Dynasty.

别梦楼后次前韵却寄

姚 鼐

送子挐舟趁晚晴，

沙边暝立听桡声，

百年身世同云散，

一夜江山共月明。

宝筏先登开觉路，

锦笺余习且多情。

钁头半个容吾与，

莫道空林此会轻。

After Saying Goodbye to Menglou I Write This Poem with the Rhyme of My Last One

Yao Nai

the sky has cleared this evening
and I come to say farewell to my friend

I stand on the beach in silence
the mooring line for his barge in my hands

listening to the swirling water
the crew bent to the oars and the craft pulled out

all the stories we wanted to tell are finished
they are vanished like dispersing clouds

but the river and the mountains
share the same bright moon on this night

your Treasure Raft teaching the scriptures
paves the Way of Awareness

but I am not so detached from the world
wanting to brush my poems on the finest paper

and the faith in Zen Buddhism we share
it is only half of the Hoe Story I understand

yet you believe all is empty in Buddhism
the meeting with you at the temple is precious

Menglou was Wang Wenzhi (1730–1802), from Dantu, Jiangsu Province.
He was a famous Chinese calligrapher and a poet. Treasure Raft is a term
in Buddhism indicating the way the Buddha taught. Way of Awareness is a
Buddhist term that means the process of understanding Buddhism. The
Hoe Story is about a disciple Dongshan got sudden awareness in the Zen
Buddhism while hoeing vegetables with his master.

望罗浮

翁方纲

只有蒙蒙意，

人家与钓矶。

寺门钟乍起，

樵客径犹非。

四百层泉落，

三千丈翠飞。

与谁参画理？

半面尽斜晖。

Looking at Luofu Mountain

Weng Fanggang

this world is shrouded in mist
a few houses and projecting rocks are visible

somewhere the temple bells ring in the dusk
woodcutter's trails are hard to tell

water from mountain springs races high and low
 from over four hundred layers

waterfalls are rushing in a glitter of emerald
three hundred thousand feet down

who is talented enough to paint this scene
half of the mountain shines in the slanting sun

Luofu Mountain is in the southeast of Guangdong Province.

村　饮

黎　简

村饮家家醵酒钱，

竹枝篱外野棠边。

谷丝久倍寻常价，

父老休谈少壮年。

细雨人归芳草晚，

东风牛藉落花眠。

秧苗已长桑芽短，

忙甚春分寒食天。

Village Drinking

Li Jian

each family gives money for the wine
villagers drink together after the long day

they meet beside the birchleaf pear trees
over there by the bamboo fencing

well they have the usual complains
how expensive the rice and raw silk is now
they ask old timers not to tell their folks again
how much better things are in their day

and maybe the rain starts in the late evening
and they walk home through the fragrant grass

and the cattle sleep in the east wind
lying on the blossoms fallen all around

and the seedlings are growing well

though the mulberry shoots have a way to go

it is a good time for farming at the equinox

families are so busy around Cold Food Day

Cold Food Day is the day before Qingming Festival. It is a festival for having cold meals only to avoid using fire in memory of a hero — Jie Zitui who was burned to death when the emperor ordered the mountain set on fire hoping to get this well-known hermit out so that he could honor him because Jie Zitui once saved the emperor's life.

二月十三夜梦于邕江上

黎　简

因友人归舟作书，寄妇梁雪。百端集于笔下。才书"家贫出门，使卿独居"八字，以风浪大作，触舟而醒。呜呼！梦而不见，不如其勿梦也，况予多病少眠，梦亦不易得耶。辄作诗寄之，得五绝句云尔。

（选一）

一度花时两梦之，

一回无语一相思。

相思坟上种红豆，

豆熟打坟知不知？

Dreaming at the Night on the Thirteenth Day of the Second Month in the Lunar Calendar in the Yongjiang River

Li Jian

I dreamed that I was writing a letter to my wife Liang Xue as a friend's boat was leaving for my hometown and he could bring the letter to her. I felt I had so much to say but I was shaken awake by the push of wind and waves against my boat. I only finished eight words in my dream: "I had to travel to make a living and this made you be left at home alone." Oh, I didn't even see her in my dream. It was no good to have such a dream. However, I have been sick for a long time and it's hard to fall asleep so that a dream is precious. What I can do now is only to write poems for her. Here the five poems are.(select one)

this spring with all those flowers in bloom
I dreamed of you twice

we did not talk for the first time
and the last time I did not even see you

I will plant a red bean shrub on your grave

with lovesickness I wait till seeds get ripe

when the red beans fall

will you hear the knock on your grave

癸巳除夕偶成 (之一)

黄景仁

千家笑语漏迟迟，

忧患潜从物外知。

悄立市桥人不识，

一星如月看多时。

At the Chinese New Year's Eve, 1773 (No. 1)

Huang Jingren

thousands of homes are filled with laughter

even though the night is getting late

and somehow I feel from nowhere

misery is coming before we are aware

I stand on the bridge alone and silent

no one in this world knows who I am

I stare so long at one bright star

it turns to face me like a withered moon

都门秋思 (之三)

黄景仁

五剧车声隐若雷，

北邙惟见冢千堆。

夕阳劝客登楼去，

山色将秋绕郭来。

寒甚更无修竹倚，

愁多思买白杨栽。

全家都在风声里，

九月衣裳未剪裁。

Thoughts on Autumn on the Gate Tower of the Capital (No. 3)

Huang Jingren

cartwheels make an incessant racket
on all the highways into the capital

but on the hillside is a cemetery
there are only graves that I see

the gate tower glows crimson
and bathed in the light of the sundown

visitors climb up the tower
because the scene is so inviting

all the mountains seem to be closer
their haze in autumn is reaching the city

there are no supple bamboos to lean against

as it is colder here than in the south

the times are so sad

I may plant more poplars in a graveyard

a cold wind blows over my whole family

how will I find winter clothes for them

绮怀 (之十六)

黄景仁

露槛星房各悄然，

江湖秋枕当游仙。

有情皓月怜孤影，

无赖闲花照独眠。

结束铅华归少作，

屏除丝竹入中年。

茫茫来日愁如海，

寄语羲和快著鞭。

Thoughts of Love (*No. 16*)

Huang Jingren

the house is quiet now under starlight

the rails in the porch bathed in dew

my dreams take me to all lands and water

as if I shift my head on an enchanted pillow

the bright moon is a fountain of emotion

its beams shadow me a lonely man with pity

and the idle flowers are so annoying

bothering me while I sleep alone

all the love poems I wrote in the early years

they were pretty verses a youth managed

no more bamboo flutes and plucked strings

I am a man who has come to midlife

and I know the sadness in my future

will be as limitless as the sea is

I sent a message to Xihe

that powerful charioteer of the sun

I urge him to whip his horses to a frenzy

and make them gallop faster and faster

Xihe is the driver of the horse pulled carriage for the sun in Chinese mythology.

山行杂诗

黄景仁

行行度深樾，

自顾不见影。

一风吹我衣，

百体共凄警。

平生轻路心，

内反犹耿耿。

虚气一相乘，

壮志不可骋。

论事贵及身，

此理庶堪省。

Poems Composed While Hiking in the Mountains

Huang Jingren

deeper and deeper into the forest
there is no light left for my shadow

the wind slaps my coat
my body shakes me to make me alert

rough roads never concerned me
now I see how dangerous they are

once you give way to your pride
your chances at a worthy goal are gone

it is worthy in our daily life
applying our thoughts of nature to ourselves

芦 沟

张问陶

芦沟南望尽尘埃，

木脱霜寒大漠开。

天海诗情驴背得，

关山秋色雨中来。

茫茫阅世无成局，

碌碌因人是废才。

往日英雄呼不起，

放歌空吊古金台。

Lugou

Zhang Wentao

all the way to the south from Lugou Bridge

there is nothing but the haze of autumn

the frost came and the leaves fell

and the land was vast and wasted

the inspiration for composing about this world

I can get it from my travels on the back of my donkey

now rain burnishes the fall colors

the hills and valleys glisten

I have spent my time in the capital

but nothing good came of my experience

now I am a man who has no purpose

someone who depends on help to get by

this place has had its heroes
and I can call on these great men

but they never answer
never quicken in my summons

there is no point in singing now
making a poem for this ancient Gold Stage

Lugou is at the Sanggan River in Hebei Province. **Gold Stage** was built by King Yanzhao in the Warring States Period, on which he displayed a large quantity of gold as his reward for talented people who would come to work for his kingdom.

阳湖道中

张问陶

风回五两月逢三,

双桨平拖水蔚蓝。

百分桃花千分柳,

冶红妖翠画江南。

Traveling through Yanghu County

Zhang Wentao

it is a pleasant day in March
feathers on the post top indicate the east wind

we do not need to use oars in this current
we let our boat drift in the blue water

the water is sprinkled with peach blossoms
drifting under the overhanging willows

peach red and willow green are so attractive
they paint the south of the Yangtze River

Yanghu is now the Changzhou County in Jiangsu Province. The Yangtze River is Changjiang.

灵泉寺

陈 沆

万树结一绿，

苍然成此山，

行入山际寺，

树外疑无天。

我心忽荡漾，

照见三灵泉。

泉性定且清，

物形视所迁。

流行与坎止，

外内符自然。

一杯且消渴，

吾意不在禅。

The Spiritual Spring Temple

Chen Hang

trees blend by the thousands into one deep green
a solidity of color sculpts the mountain

entering this mysterious place there is the temple
I cannot imagine there is a sky above this forest

suddenly my heart quickens
and I have come to the well called Spiritual Spring

this spring is so clear and calm as if it were empty
it fills its basin with water but scarcely murmurs

water reflects the nature of this world
forms the shape of the place where it runs or stops

I just want a cup of water from this well

to slake my thirst at this moment

I am not speaking of Zen Buddhism

Spiritual Spring Temple is in the south of Zigui County, Hubei Province, which was named after the well called Spiritual Spring, in front of the temple, half way up the hill. The water in the well rises and falls according to the rise and fall of the water in the Yangtze River.

赴戍登程口占示家人 (之二)

林则徐

力微任重久神疲，

再竭衰庸定不支，

苟利国家生死以，

岂因祸福避趋之。

谪居正是君恩厚，

养拙刚于戍卒宜。

戏与山妻谈故事，

试吟断送老头皮。

A Verbally Created Poem Saying Goodbye to Family Members after Being Relegated to the West (No. 2)

Lin Zexu

I have been overwhelmed for a long time
this important office means too much for me

I am really not all an intelligent man
so if I remain here what good thing would it be

I have dedicated my life to serving the kingdom
I won't crawl into a hole when I am facing dangers

I tell you this new post is not an exile
it is really a gesture of kindness from the emperor

I will be a soldier on the border
it may be just good for a man of decency

I cheer my wife by telling that old story

how an old lady wrote a poem to warn her old man

that the old man might lose his head in jail

if he still gets drunk and recites poems madly

Lin Zexu was the commander in the First Opium War period and was finally banished from the court by the emperor. **That old story:** Lin Zexu put a note to this poem himself about that old story, in which a hermit poet was asked to meet the emperor in the Song Dynasty and told the emperor that his wife wrote a poem to him to advise him not to drink and read aloud poems otherwise his head might be cut off. In history, poet Su Shi was once under arrest by emperor's order, and his wife cried while seeing Su Shi off. Su Shi made his wife laugh by asking her to write a poem to him like that lady in that story.

西郊落花歌

龚自珍

西郊落花天下奇,

古来但赋伤春诗。

西郊车马一朝尽,

定盦先生沽酒来赏之。

先生探春人不觉,

先生送春人又嗤。

呼朋亦得三四子,

出城失色神皆痴。

如钱塘潮夜澎湃,

如昆阳战晨披靡;

如八万四千天女洗脸罢,

齐向此地倾胭脂。

奇龙怪凤爱漂泊；

琴高之鲤何反欲上天为？

玉皇宫中空若洗，

三十六界无一青峨眉；

又如先生平生之忧患，

恍惚怪诞百出难穷期。

先生读书尽三藏，

最喜《维摩》卷里多清词。

又闻净土落花深四寸，

瞑目观想尤神驰。

西方净国未可到，

下笔绮语何漓漓！

安得树有不尽之花更雨新好者，

三百六十日长是落花时！

Song for the Falling Blossoms
in the Western Suburbs of Beijing

Gong Zizhen

they are wonders of the world really

these blossoms fallen in the western suburbs

people have written sad poems

since the old days about the loss of spring

no horses and carriages come sightseeing

when the blossoms are over and done with

but I invite my friends to come with me

and enjoy these blooms while drinking wine

no one will know we are here

and if someone did he would laugh at us

still the three or four I call

they are astonished when they come out of the city

piles of these blossoms seem like great waves
cresting at the mouth of Qiantang River

they seem like the four hundred thousand soldiers
being routed and dispersed in the Kunyang battle

they are a rinsing of cosmetic colors
that eighty-four thousand sylphs poured from heaven

they look like strange dragons and phoenixes
that drop down and flow through the air

even that winged carp leaps up to the sky
with the lucky guy Qin Gao clinging to its back

they are those sylphs having emptied the heaven
hurrying down from all the thirty-six levels

they are so unexpected and so endless in the sky
they are like all the ups and downs in my life

I've read all the three Buddhist Scriptures
the most interesting words are from *Vimalakirti Sutra*

I have heard of the pure land of the Buddha
where fallen blossoms pile up over five inches high

oh I close my eyes and dream of such a place
and how I might reach that paradise in the west

and yet here my writing is full of loving words
breaking the strict rules of the Buddha

I wish more blossoms would fall down
they would look fresher and prettier

in the year of some three hundred and sixty days

there would be falling blossoms from morning till night

The Qiantang River is in Zhejiang Province. The rising tide from the sea rushes into the mouth of the Qiantang River pushing the river current back to create huge waves. Kunyang is in Ye County, He'nan Province, where the battle between Liu Xiu and Wang Mang took place in 23 AD, with ten thousand soldiers on one side and four hundred thousand soldiers on the other. Eighty -four thousand is from Buddhist Scripture indicating very many. Qin Gao climbed up onto the back of a ten feet long carp in the field and the carp took off flying into the sky in Chinese legend. Thirty-six levels is from Taoist Scripture. It implies that there are thirty-six levels of sky between human's earth and god's heaven. Writing loving words is one of the ten sins in Buddhism.

己亥杂诗 (之一百二十五)

龚自珍

九州风气恃风雷，

万马齐喑究可哀。

我劝天公重抖擞，

不拘一格降人才。

Random Poems from 1839 *(No. 125)*

Gong Zizhen

the vitality of China can only be unleashed
with shuddering thunder and high wind

what a pity there is no steed making battle screams
that would break the silence

may the heavens come alive again
listen to my call for the great power of creation

may the heavens send us remarkable men
with all kinds of sharp talents and keen abilities

己亥杂诗 (之二百二十一)

龚自珍

西墙枯树态纵横,

奇古全凭一臂撑。

烈士暮年宜学道。

江关词赋笑兰成。

Random Poems from 1839 *(No. 221)*

Gong Zizhe

this old and withered tree
still holds these gnarled branches
against the western wall

it is hard to believe
such a mass of twisted limbs
could balance on one trunk

a man with a noble goal
would stand upright for truth
even if age bents him double

I am not in favor of Lan Cheng

who wrote sad poems in his late years

all his miserable life and homesickness

Lan Cheng (Yu Xin) was an ambassador of the Liang Kingdom, staying in the North Kingdom. Later he was not allowed to go back home in the south when his Liang Kingdom was conquered. He wrote a lot of sad poems in his late years.

三湘棹歌

魏 源

溪山雨后湘烟起,

杨柳愁杀鹭鸥喜。

棹歌一声天地绿,

回首浯溪已十里。

雨前方恨湘水平,

雨后又嫌湘水奔。

浓于酒更碧于云,

熨不能平剪不分。

水复山重行未尽,

压来七十二峰影。

篙篙打碎碧玉屏,

家家汲得桃花井。

Boatman's Song in Three Xiang Rivers: the Zhengxiang River

Wei Yuan

after the rain on Xi Mountain
the fog drifts over the Zhengxiang River

poplar and willow
droop sadly beneath the showers

but the heron and the gulls
revel in the damp air and the rising water

it seems with just one line of the boatman's song
this world has changed into a green haven

I look back to glimpse the Wuxi River
but already it is miles upstream

the Xiang water was too calm before the rain

and now it is a torrent purling between its banks

a freshet is more heady than plum wine
purer and clearer than high clouds

you cannot flatten it like ironing a piece of cloth
or cut its unruly current by using a pair of scissors

my boat winds through the mountain valleys
and sails over the seventy-two peaks reflected in water

the dip of the barge pole
disturbs a jade-green water

families dip up these peach blossomed waters
as if the water is from wells in their courtyards

This poem is mimicking the boatman's song in the area of Dongting
Lake in Hu'nan Province where three rivers run into this lake. **The Zhengxiang
River** is one of Three Xiang Rivers, along which there are seventy-two peaks
of Mountain Hengshan. **The Wuxi** is a river running from north through the
southwest of Qiyang County in Hu'nan Province into the Xiang River.

经死哀

郑　珍

虎卒未去虎隶来，

催纳捐欠声如雷。

雷声不住哭声起，

走报其翁已经死。

长官切齿目怒瞋：

"吾不要命只要银。

若图作鬼即宽减，

恐此一县无生人！"

促呼捉子来，

且与杖一百：

"陷父不义罪何极，

欲解父悬速足陌！"

呜呼！

北城卖屋虫出户，

南城又报缢三五。

Mourning Those Who Hanged Themselves
Zheng Zhen

the troops of tax collectors

came roaring like tigers

and when one troop abandoned the town

another came beating on the doors like thunder

shouting pay your taxes

the people started crying in despair

but the pounding on the door never ceased

the son went to tell his father

and the father hanged himself there

the chief official stared at them

with cold fury in his eyes

and clenched his teeth noisily

I didn't want lives he shouted I want silver

If you were exempted from taxes because of his death

I am afraid there would be no one alive in this county

then he had the son of the family seized
and had him be flogged one hundred slashes

the tax collector shouted
what a criminal you are
you put your father in unrighteousness
I tell you your father's body will hang there
until his taxes are paid to the last penny

oh the misery was tremendous
in the north of the town
a dead man's house was for sale
while worms crawling out of the house
from the rotting body hanging in the air

and then from the south more news came
a few more fathers hanged themselves

哀旅顺

黄遵宪

海水一泓烟九点，

壮哉此地实天险。

炮台屹立如虎阚，

红衣大将威望俨。

下有洼池列巨舰，

晴天雷轰夜电闪。

最高峰头纵远览，

龙旗百丈迎风飐。

长城万里此为堑，

鲸鹏相摩图一啖。

昂头侧睨视眈眈，

伸手欲攫终不敢。

谓海可填山易撼，

万鬼聚谋无此胆。

一朝瓦解成劫灰，

闻道敌军蹈背来。

Mourning Lüshun

Huang Zunxian

this harbor is a great natural bowl
and the passage into it is a narrow channel

it was once an excellent fortress for China
an impenetrable natural defense

it was on the hills above
crouched like a tiger which was ready to roar

it had a cannon called the Warrior in Red
that was an engine of profound terror

powerful warships rode at anchor
secure in the waters below

the cannon cracked with thunder in the day
and flashed with lightening in the darkened sky

you could watch with a bird's view on the peak
the long rows of dragon banners snapping in the wind

this harbor was like the moat of the Great Wall
any attempt to invade China came to a halt here

those mighty world powers
the ones that would wolf down China

they could only stare with envy at this harbor
and keep their thieving hands in their pockets

as said it's easy to fill the seas and shake mountains
but those powers would not dare challenge this place

once they learned that the Japanese army had come
through the mountains in the back of the fortress

then all the defenses were burned to ashes

resistance crushed in a wink

The war depicted in this poem was between Japan and China in 1894. China lost the war. The military harbor **Lüshun** in Liaoning Province was captured by Japanese on November 21 that year. The poet wrote this poem right after that.

出都留别诸公

康有为

天龙作骑万灵从，

独立飞来缥缈峰。

怀抱芳馨兰一握，

纵横宙合雾千重。

眼中战国成争鹿，

海内人才孰卧龙？

抚剑长号归去也，

千山风雨啸青锋。

A Poem to Say Goodbye While Leaving the Capital

Kang Youwei

I would ride the back of a dragon from heaven
flying in the sky followed by all the gods

stand alone on top of this mountain
it was said that it flew here from India

and I try my best to follow the noble ancestors
but beneath my gaze is all mist and fog

all the great powers of this world
struggle to possess my beloved land

what can you do when those with talent
have to live in seclusion like Zhuge Liang

I would leave howling and stroking my sword
and my sword would growl in the wind and rain

the driven rain comes crashing down
over the mountains and valleys of the earth

Kang Youwei was the vanguard promoting political reform of the system in the Qing Dynasty. He submitted the written statement to the emperor in 1888 and then left the capital in September, 1889. He himself put a note to the poems: "I presented to the imperial court my proposal to introduce institutional reforms. It never happened in the history of China, but it has been under massive suspicion. So I left." **Zhuge Liang** was the premier of the Shu Kingdom in the Three Kingdoms Period. He was a reclusive talent in Longzhong, today's Xiangyang, Hubei Province before he was invited to be the chief. He established the Shu Kindom in today's Chengdu, Sichuan Province and maintained the stable situation of the co-existence of the Three kingdoms.

丙申之冬入天津，泊己亥秋始得归，将行，赋此二律（之一）

夏曾佑

鸿飞本不为留计，

竟见荒原万瓦稠。

又举离觞辞旧雨，

为思身世怯登楼。

青山白浪驰黄海，

细雨疏灯过秀州。

从此归帆好云物，

分明点点入新愁。

Leaving Tianjin after the Stay of Three Years 1896–1899 (No. 1)

Xia Zengyou

geese fly but don't care where they will be
they know they don't linger anywhere

but I was surprised to see so many houses
where there was nothing when I first came

I raise my cup
and say goodbye to old friends

I hesitate to climb the steps of a pagoda
where all the sorrows will return to me

my boat will hurry along the Yellow Sea
the green mountains and white waves

through the incessant rain

and will pass the scattered light in Xiuzhou

my old skies and my clouds they will be wonderful

but I know they will bring me new sorrow

Xia Zengyou was one of the founders of the National News which was very popular in pushing the political reform under the support of Emperor Guangxu. The poet left Tianjin in 1899 after the reform movement failed and many of the reformers were persecuted and sentenced. Xiuzhou is now Jiaxing, in Zhejiang Province.

晨登衡岳祝融峰

谭嗣同

身高殊不觉，

四顾乃无峰。

但有浮云度，

时时一荡胸。

地沉星尽没，

天跃日初熔。

半勺洞庭水，

秋寒欲起龙。

Climbing Zhurong Peak of Hengyue Mountain at Daybreak

Tan Sitong

I scarcely know how high up I am
as when I look around there are no peaks

clouds float and pass by now and then
I'm so inspired and ambitious once I breathe

the earth seems to be sinking below me
and even at this moment the stars vanish

the morning sky burns red with the sunrise
the sun glows jumping out of a furnace

the Dongting Lake seems only a half spoon of water
the dragon in it will have to soar up as it gets chilly in fall

---

Hengyue Mountain is in the east of Hu'nan Province and has five major peaks. Zhurong Peak is one of Hengyue Mountain's peaks. The Dongting Lake is in Hu'nan Province.

读陆放翁集 (之一)

梁启超

诗界千年靡靡风，

兵魂销尽国魂空。

集中什九从军乐，

亘古男儿一放翁。

Reading the Collection of Poems
by Lu Fangweng (No. 1)

Liang Qichao

obscenity has been the style

in the poetry world for a thousand years

decadence prevails over the country

the ancient martial spirit is dead

nine out of ten of his poems say joining up

breathing with the old fighting spirit

we can't find such a man like Lu Fangweng

from the old days in our long history

The poet Liang Qichao wrote a note to this poem himself: "All Chinese poets wrote about the hardships of being an army man but poet **Lu Fangweng (Lu You)** was an exception, who admired the spirit of soldiers, dying for their country until his very late years."

本事诗十章 (之九)

苏曼殊

春雨楼头尺八箫，

何时归看浙江潮？

芒鞋破钵无人识，

踏过樱花第几桥？

Ten Poems from Moments in My Life (No. 9)

Su Manshu

spring rain falls over the corner of this building
sad music echoes there from a Chiba bamboo flute

when will I be able to go home
see the tide roar up the Qiantang River

no one knows me a monk wearing straw sandals
and holding a broken begging bowl

I don't know how many bridges I have crossed
all covered with fallen cherry blossoms

The poet was a Chinese monk who traveled to Japan in January, 1909 and fell in love with a geisha in Tokyo. All the ten poems were about his love story. The Chiba is a type of flute in Japan. Qiantang River is in Zhejiang Province. The rising tide from the sea rushed into the mouth of Qiantang River pushing the river current back to create huge waves.

后 记

—— 与文化共舞:中国古典诗词英译

英译中国从唐朝到清朝（618—1911）古典诗词的工程后半部分,经过几十年的工作不辍,终告完成,深感欣慰。这后半部分覆盖了中国元、明、清三个朝代(1206—1911),书名为:《归舟:中国元明清诗选》。

我感到高兴,不仅是因为这个工程已经完成,而且还因为这个翻译的过程。在翻译过程中,我和我的合作者、著名美国诗人约翰·诺弗尔得到一个与两种不同的文化共舞的机会。我们感到这两种文化就像两个翅膀,让我们升到空中享受文学翻译的自由。

有些翻译界同行感到文学翻译简直就是带着镣铐跳舞,我对此深表同情。同时我也感知到同行们虽然这样说,可是并不是道辛苦,而是为此感到骄傲。在17世纪初,一位非常重要的英国诗人兼翻译家约翰·德莱顿(1631—1700)也曾用这样的比喻对进行"字对字,行对行"的翻译的同行表示同情,他在他英译的《奥维德书信》(1680年)的前言中写道,逐字翻译"很像双脚带着镣铐在绳子上跳舞"(露丝亚·V.阿兰达,2007年),这成为翻译批评家们常常引用的话。

我感到学术圈一直对建立翻译标准感兴趣,可是那永远不会成功,对文学翻译来说就更难成功。建立一套文学翻译的规则,并且尝试使它成为权威，尝试用这套翻译规则来评断一个译家及其译作，必定劳而无功。大多数情形下，一个译家写出自己在翻译中的经验、心得是为了与同行们分享，没有建立规范让译家们去效法的意思。译家公开这些个人想法和观点的唯一理由就是供文学翻译批评家去探讨、评论，因为他们的讨论很可能会使一个译家的见解得到更好的分享。

严复的故事是一个很好的例子。他在1896年翻译了托马斯·亨利·赫胥黎的《天演论》，并在1898年将其出版，那时赫胥黎先生已经去世了。他在这本译著的前言里指出三个难题："信""达""雅"。那完全不是训诫。我的理解是，从某种意义上说，严复尝试表达他的懊恼，即未能彻底克服这三个难题，他还进一步解释了他在翻译中由于选择的局限而导致的一些麻烦。

其实，严复是一位真诚的译家，坦率地承认自己的经验的三个难题难以克服。我想这是切实的经验之谈，非常有助于后来的译家的翻译实践。他亲身体验到，为了避免原作者的观点与自己的理论分析发生抵触，他不得不砍掉所译原书的后一半；为了使译文能有所用，又不得不根据自己的需求把原书分割成三十五章，以便加上自拟的标题，进而对其中二十八章逐章加上自己的评论，在评论中将原著的理论与中国的社会问题和社会现实相联系。这可能就是他感叹在翻译中做到"信"之难的原委。

严复先生感叹"达"之难也有其原因。他认为译家只要弄懂了原文，就可以用译入语中的任何自己想用的语言材料，使译文富于表达力即可。这难免会让译家的创作欲望膨胀，信马由缰，一展身手；我想他一定又担心，如此之"达"难免又会有远离"信"的可能。

严复先生认为，"雅"就是要选用最优雅的文字、最优雅的文风，而且非先秦的文字与文风莫属。秦朝(公元前221—公元前206)比他生活的时代早约两千年。他笃信越是伟大的理论越是要用中国最优雅的文字和文风来翻译，因为伟大的理论只是给那些有才能的人阅读的，并非给普通人阅读。他判断有文化但是不经常阅读古典书籍的人，应该也无法读懂译文。由此看来，严复先生将"雅"作为翻译的三个困难之一的经验完全来自他对自己高标准的要求，又担心做得不到位；他对读者以高标准要求，又忧其不能。从历史事实来看，当时的文人雅士、改革派人士、革命党人，无一不在捧读他翻译的《天演论》；翻译界的人士，无一不读他为《天演论》写的前言。

认真地说，我没有责怪的意思，我认为严复所写的那篇前言没有什么不当。那篇前言通篇只是他尝试与人们分享他的关于翻译的经验和观点，而这些经验和观点有可能对其他译家有参考价值。如果他没有译好，也只是他自己的问题，与其他译家毫无关联。我做了上述对严复所列举的三点翻译的难处的分析，只是为了提醒人们，我们不应当用他写的这篇前言建立起标准，用以约束所有翻译工作。事实上，一百多年来，人们已经把严复所列举的三项翻译难处变成了严格的翻译规则。这使几代译者在其后续的影响中饱受其苦。此外，他的经验只是来自科学著作翻译，甚至不是来自社会科学著作翻译，也不是来自文学著作翻译，当然更不是在翻译诗歌的过程中获得的，当然具有局限性。在没有极强的学术分类和对术语的准确界定的情况下，个人的翻译经验是不可能被考虑作为一种规范的。如果我们已经给自己带上了沉重枷锁，那就让我们把它抖掉吧。

经过这番澄清之后，我觉得我可以谈谈我在翻译中国古典诗词中的心得体会。人人都知道，翻译是高度个体化的，没有任何两个译家所谈的经验是相同的，甚至在翻译相同诗歌的情况下也是如此。文学翻译经验的繁复多样正是文学翻译的丰富多彩的表现。在《唐诗选》和《宋诗词选》两本英译本于美国出版后，我写了一篇关于我在英译中国古典诗词过程中的心得体会：《从差异中寻求连接点——古诗词英译的诗美追求》（《外语学刊》，1986年第4期）。在这个基础上，我又写了另一篇题为《中国古诗词英译刍议》的论文，于1987年12月在香港当代翻译研讨会上宣读，这篇论文后来被发表（《外国语》，1988年第4期）。这两篇论文都尝试强调文学翻译对文化的关注。我现在所写的这篇后记，仍然意在强调文学翻译对文化关照的需求。一般地讲，翻译是跨文化的。可是具体地说，文学翻译是在与两种不同文化的表征打交道，因为文学是文化的载体，同时也是文化的符号。

进一步说，诗歌的翻译应该是为了把诗歌送达目的语读者和目的文化中的读者，他们是接受主体，根据接受美学的理论（汉斯·罗伯特·吉奥思，1967年），接受主体参与欣赏才把文本转化成为文学作品。如果译家忽略这样一个现实——这些读者作为接受主体在完全不同的文化当中成长，那么译家的文本在接受主体看来是模糊不清的，他们就完全不可能对其进行欣赏。当他们不再理睬你的译文，不愿意或者没有能力参与完成作品创作的最后一个环节，那么翻译文本就会失去从翻译文本升华成文学作品的机会。这样一来，译家就无法完成把原语诗歌介绍到目的语中的任务，而且也堵死了原语诗人走进另一种文化中的读者群体的路径。

在这样一种诚惶诚恐的阴影笼罩下，我试图弄明白在技术上我能做到什么和我不能做到什么。一个文学翻译家的最基本的智慧应该是清楚地意识到翻译的局限性。其他的事情,诸如对两种语言的掌握、关于文学的知识、诗歌写作的技巧等,都是第二位的。中国古典诗词翻译的目的就是要把中国古代凝聚着丰富文化的文学瑰宝介绍给那些说英语的读者。翻译者希望做到让读者能够欣赏这些诗歌,能够体验到诗的激情、启迪,从文字到感受的传递和情感的满足。这些是通过我们的努力能够做到的。读者甚至可能产生到中国旅游、学习中文、参观诗中所描写的那些景点的兴致,这些也是我所关心的。

现在我们可以看到:一位译家受到原语的诗人的极大信任,他们不懂目的语;一位译家也受到目的语读者的极大信任,他们不懂原语。跨文化的交际就完全依赖于译家。译家必须能够驾驭两种语言,必须能真诚地对待这两部分人,必须做出巨大的努力,在两种不同的文化中找到那个能实现连接的点,从那里完成文化的超越。翻译家的真诚至关重要,只有真诚才是最重要的。

文学翻译家必须对原语诗人真诚。接受美学理论认为,在诗歌批评中,诗人本人并不重要。但是对于一位诗歌译者来说,他深知诗人的人生是绝对重要的。这将使译者触及诗人的情感和诗人投入到一首特定的诗歌里的独特的情绪。诗人的个人生活,包括他的家庭、爱情、苦难、政治失意和属于某一个风格流派这个事实等等,会对发掘诗的意义有所帮助。意义是诗歌最能触动读者的一个方面。有时意义又是通过象征的含蓄、意象、传说、神话来传达的,可是这些常常是很难"啃"的。如果你深知这位诗人,你就不需要用自己的臆想来破解这首诗。有了对诗的彻底理解,你的翻译才能像原著一样具有魅力。

译家应当有这种感受：他是在和诗人一同翻译，或者是在代表那些人已不在、已经无力保卫他们的诗歌文本的诗人们进行翻译。译家必须确切知道诗人到底要告诉人们什么，以此为据，才能在众多的选择前做出这正确的选择。如果做出不恰当的选择，译家就会让原语诗歌受到损害。

译家必须对原语诗歌真诚。不管多难，文学翻译家都要竭尽其能地译出诗意、情绪、内蕴、文化内涵、意象、象征、典故和品质。这不只是修辞问题。我判断，如果我们能把这些事情做好，我们就对诗歌真诚了，不亏欠诗人。不管怎样不方便，我们都应该穷尽一切努力去避免砍掉原诗中的主要信息、替代原诗中的元素、忽略诗中用典或对文化内涵完全置之不顾。作为一个文学翻译者，我从不设置自己的规则来限制翻译或者强行让自己的翻译去适应一种预设的模式。相反，我设法调整自己以忠实再现原诗。我愿意冒着难以说出正当理由的风险放弃中国古典诗词的形式。我的理解是把中国古典诗词的格式套入英国古典诗歌的模式，只能得到与中国古典诗词格式相似的作品。它们永远不能一致。可是，相似并非相同，译作并非原品，不幸的是它倒可能成为赝品。我宁愿放弃这种格式也不愿意看到翻译因硬搬格式而受到损害。

中国古典诗歌有它自成系统的格律，它严格地限定每一个韵律诗行的长短，每一行具有相同的字数，限定每一个诗节中所包含的行数，也限定一首诗中应有几个诗节。这个系统为了达到音乐效果还设定了严格的格式：由于每个汉字都有四个声调，在每一个特定诗行里的每一个特定位置上都只能用一个有某种声调的字，在每两个紧邻的诗行里，在特定的位置上，两行的用字要根据字的四声按照格式对应平仄。除此之外，在两个平行对仗的诗行中，相同位置上的词语要在音调、词的表面意义和词的内涵意义上都相互对偶。可是这些对偶的词又必须是同一词性、同一类别的词。此外，在第一个诗节里，这两个对偶的诗行，必须是第三行和第四行；而在第二个诗节里，必须是第一行与第二行。而且，在两个诗节之间，上一节的最后一行与下一节的第一行之间，也要做到相同位置上的词的四声根据格式相互对应。对于押韵的要求也是严格的。在一首八行的诗里，第二行、第四行、第六行必须是押韵的；在一首四行的诗里，第二行、第四行必须是押韵的。这是一种非常复杂而令人感叹的诗歌形式，盛而不衰近一千五百年。

实际上，印在这本书里的中国古典诗歌的外部结构已经被现代化了。在古代的中国，诗并不是被分成短行来书写的，而是被写成像散文一样的一篇，不使用任何标点符号。它们是被由上到下书写的，换行是从右向左。印在这本书里的中国古典诗歌，其外部形式已经被大幅度改变，但是它容易被接受，因为它符合现代中国人的阅读习惯，我相信，这也是目的语读者所习惯的形式。在英译时，中国古诗词的形式只是一种表层的东西而已。

然而随着时间的流逝，在20世纪初，这些格式和规则已经在中国的诗歌写作中被放弃了。从那时起，中国诗人已经用自由体写诗近一个世纪了。为什么我们的译作要回到被放弃的形式呢？我并不想去说明在英语翻译中保持这种形式是不可能的，但是我在提请人们的注意，这样翻译是很容易给诗的意义和诗的想象造成损害的。

这种对古老的格律形式和古老的押韵形式的摈弃也发生在英

语诗歌中。世界在不断地变化，而我们写作诗歌的方式也在改变。英语诗人写作自由诗已有百年的历史了，始于20世纪初美国的新诗运动。

自由诗并非写成短行的散文，而是每一行都有它自己的音乐品质。当然,它没有人人都必须遵守的格式。我经常把我们的英译诗歌高声地读给我的合作译者约翰·诺弗尔听，他也高声地读给我听。我们小心翼翼地互相倾听,目的是要确定我们的译诗听起来有诗的韵味。如果听起来不好，我们会重新来过。虽然我们从不按照某种事先规定的韵律和格式来译诗，但是我们都陶醉于每一行诗的音乐感。我希望我们的英语读者也会高声朗读我们的译诗，以欣赏翻译成英语自由体的诗歌的音乐美感。如果能这样，我认为我们做到了对原语诗歌的真诚。

文学翻译家必须忠实于目的语和目的文化中的读者。从某种意义上看,读者就是译家的主顾。翻译的目的是让原语诗歌走进另一种文化，这是尽人皆知的。翻译的诗歌在目的语读者听来可能是外国的，但是它必须是目的语读者能读的、能接受的、能感受到吸引力的。翻译的诗歌一定是由目的语读者来鉴赏的，而不是由翻译者来鉴赏的。如果目的语读者不喜欢这译诗,这样的译诗就没有前景可言。

有了这样一个信念，我们就不会黏住已不再被使用的中国古典诗歌的形式不放，也不会一定要把译诗套进已经不再被使用的英语古典诗歌的形式。这样套用的后果是很可能又创造出一种新的诗歌形式,它既不能准确地反映出中国古典诗歌的形式,也不吻合英语古典诗歌的形式。我们应当明白，每当一种形式被放弃了，就是读者对这种形式厌倦了。这恐怕是中国古典诗歌的形式和英语古典诗歌的形式被摈弃的唯一原因吧。译家应该清楚,尝试去保留古典诗歌的形式只是一种认为死去的形式还可以再生的幻觉。

有的译家在再现中国古典诗歌的形式时走得更远,为了让原诗有可能被套进译家所设想的模式,对原诗实施删减、替代和忽略。毫无疑问,这样做会给原诗的精髓和意义带来损害。在一些翻译中,删减、替代和忽略已经成为让原诗适应译家所设计的形式的司空见惯的手法,读者得不到提醒、得不到解释、得不到道歉,甚至也看不到一个简单的注。这种情形下,译家滥用了他所拥有的权力,因为原语诗人依赖于译家,目的语读者也依赖于译家。当译家为此所困,认为可以想怎样做就怎样做,他就陷进泥淖之中。因为总是有很多人,他们既掌握目的语又掌握原语且又懂得诗歌,他们将成为目的语读者的帮手。如果我们犯下这样的错误,我们就没有忠于读者,因为我们误导了他们。

如果译家在翻译的目的语中出现错误,译者与读者之间的关系即遭破坏,因为这会被视为比本族语的人在写作中犯错误更糟糕的事情。读者不会原谅译者,只会对译者失去信任。另一个破坏读者与译者之间的关系的因素是信息遗漏,特别是文化内涵的遗失。一旦这种情况被目的语读者发现,他们通常会得出这样的结论:这个译家不合格,因为他连诗歌和自己的母语和文化中的文学都不懂。

翻译者永远不能犯目的语语言上的错误,也不能犯目的语及原语的文化上的错误。如果我们不滥用权力,我们会翻译得更好。

文学翻译家要对自己真诚。我们必须诚实,知道我们不是诗人,我们是在翻译。很可能,我们是诗人,甚至发表过诗歌作品,但是我们不是那位写了这首我们正在翻译的诗的诗人。我们必须弄明白我们是在翻译诗，而不是在写诗。如果我们忘记了这一点，哪怕只是一瞬间，我们在翻译中的遣词造句就会立刻与我们的翻译目的背道而驰。我们的目的是把原诗的含义准确地翻译成目的语，给目的语读者以启迪和震撼，让他们实现从文字到体验的升华。选词造句总是有多种多样的内涵可供选择，也正是这种选择造就了诗人的独特的风格。一个真诚的译家总是选择能够再现原语诗人的风格的词语和修辞，而绝对不是展现译家自己的风格。

真诚的译家毫不犹豫地承认翻译的局限性，并且承认他们自己在诸多方面的局限性，相比较而言，后者更难做到。有了这样的智慧，就肯定会比较容易地弄清楚什么是我们做不到的和什么是我们不该做的。译家的直觉一定能够感觉到这底线。

一位真诚的译家要认真追寻和深入发掘的最重要的事情就是文化。拥有两种文化的广博的知识和穷尽所能地探讨可以使我们享有与两种文化共舞的自由。如果我们能实现与两种文化共舞，就能使文学翻译成为极大的享受——自由地进行跨文化交际的享受。看来具有双文化素养和具有双语素养同样大有裨益。

在后记要结束时，我想明确一下，后记里所写的完全是我在把中国古典诗词翻译成英语过程中的体会，写出来的动机就只是与人分享。我突出加强文学翻译对文化的关注、对文化的参照和对文化的认同，但是我们知道文学翻译的高度个体性，甚至可以说非常地因人而异。坦率地说，这是完全可能发生的，像一句英语谚语所说："对一个人可能是美食，对另一个人就可能是毒药"。尽管如此，分享信息总是好的。

在很多领域里,人们都倾向于用文化来解决问题。我一直认为文学翻译家只能是"文化正确"而非"技术正确"。许多不同文化中的专家、学者相信用文化来解决问题对其专业很有利。当我英译中国古诗词时,时而感到迷惘,但是我知道标准就在我置身其中的文化里。在翻译中国古诗词时,与文化共舞不仅仅是一个方法问题,它也是一条让翻译家逃离枷锁的路径。

没有一种解决方案会十全十美,但是我尝试了一种,我相信它解决了难题。

王守义

2017年9月4日

于多伦多教堂街

(本文翻译:孙苏荔　校订:王守义)

Epilogue

— Dancing with Culture: Translating Classical Chinese
Poems into English

It is a great relief to accomplish the second half of the project —
an English Translation of Classical Chinese Poems from the Tang
Dynasty to the Qing Dynasty (618–1911) as it has been worked on
for a couple of decades. The second half covers the Yuan, Ming and
Qing Dynasties (1206–1911) entitled *Voyage Home: Poems from the
Yuan and Ming and Qing Dynasties of China.*

The joy I'm feeling is not only from the completion of the project
but also from the process of the translating, which gave me and my
co-translator John Knoepfle, a well-known American poet the chance
to dance with two different cultures. We felt that the two cultures were
like two wings, which took us into the air to enjoy the freedom in
literary translation.

I sympathize with those colleagues who feel literary translation is
nothing but dancing in chains. Somehow I know they don't think that
it is a kind of hardship when they talk about it like that. I believe
they feel somewhat proud when they elaborate it that way. In the

early seventeenth century, John Dryden (1631 – 1700), an important British poet and translator sympathized with some colleagues who did the "word by word and line by line" translation and he commented on it in his preface to his translation of *Ovid's Epistles* (1680), he thought that literal translation is "much like dancing on ropes with fettered legs" (Lucia V. Aranda, 2007), critics often quote this.

I have a feeling that the academic circle has been interested in setting up standards for translation, which will never succeed, for literary translation particularly. To set up a set of rules for literary translation and even try to make it dominant and use it to judge translators and their translation will end in failure. Most of the time, a translator writes about the experience in doing translation to share with colleagues, the translator has no intention to set up some norms for translators to follow. The only reason to publicize those personal thoughts and perspectives is for literary translation critics to discuss and to review because their discussions may help one translator's insights be better shared.

A good example is the case of Yan Fu. He translated Thomas Henry Huxley's *Evolution and Ethics* in 1896 and published it in 1898. By then Mr. Huxley had passed away. The three difficulties Yan Fu named in his preface to the translated book were "faithfulness," "expressiveness," and "elegance." That is not a dictum at all. In a sense, from my reading, Yan Fu tried to express his regrets for not being able to overcome the three difficulties thoroughly and further explained some other problems in his translation due to the limitation of choice.

To be honest, Mr. Yan Fu was a sincere translator who openly exposed the three difficulties from his own experience of which he frankly admitted that it's not easy to overcome. I do believe this was genuinely from his personal practice and would be valuable for trans-lators after him. He himself experienced that in order to avoid the clash between his theoretical analysis and the viewpoint of the author, he had to cut off the second half of the book. For the purpose of making use of the book, he had to divide the text into thirty-five chapters according to his needs, so that he could create a title for each, and further for twenty-eight chapters where he wrote a comment for each one from his own point of view. He also connected, in his comments inserted, the theory in the original text with the social problems and social realities of China at that time. That could be the reason why he concluded that it was very difficult to keep to "faith-fulness" in translation.

There is also a reason for Mr. Yan Fu to pin down "expressive-ness" as the second difficulty for translators to get over. It's his understanding that a translator can use whatever words in the target language in pursuit of "expressiveness" only if the translator under-stands the original text. Possibly this will unleash a translator's desire of writing free of restrictions like riding with lax reins. I believe his concern was that such "expressiveness" may cause great deviation from "faithfulness."

As for "elegance," Mr. Yan Fu insisted on selecting the most elegant words and writing style used before the Qin Dynasty (221 BC-206 BC), two thousand years before his time. He believed that great theory deserved a translation with the most elegant words and the writing style used in ancient China. Mr. Yan Fu stressed that great theory was only for the great talent, not for the ordinary people, so that he assumed that even educated people who did not often read ancient books wouldn't be able to read his translation. It's so obvious that he named "elegance" as one of the three difficulties from his experience was due to his setting a very high standard for himself while feeling ashamed of his own inferiority and due to his setting a very high standard for his readers while feeling worried about their inability. From the historical facts we know that at his time all the men of letters, scholars, the reformists, and revolutionaries were reading his translation of *Evolution and Ethics* and all translators were reading the preface he wrote for this translated book.

Seriously, I'm not blaming Yan Fu as he didn't do anything wrong in writing that preface. On the whole, he just attempted to share his experience and his perspectives about translation with people, which could serve as reference for other translators. If he didn't do it well, that was his own problem. It has nothing to do with other translators. I did above analysis of the three difficulties he named was just to remind people that we shouldn't use the preface Yan Fu wrote to set up standards to constrain all translations. As a matter of fact, the three difficulties Yan Fu named have been turned into strict rules by people and they have followed them for more than one hundred years. Generations have suffered from its consequences. Besides, his experience was only from his translation of the scientific work, not from the social science work, not from the literary works, definitely not from poems so that this experience was surely very limited. Personal experience in translation couldn't be considered as a norm without very academic classification and accurate defining of terms. If we have put a heavy yoke on ourselves, let us shake it off.

With this clarification, I assume I can talk about my experience in translation of classical Chinese poems. Everyone knows translation is highly individual and experience from two translators, even when they both translate the same poems, the translation couldn't be the same. The variety of experiences in literary translation is a sign of richness in literary translation. After the publishing of *Tang Dynasty Poems* and *Song Dynasty Poems* in the United States, I wrote about my experience in translating classical Chinese poems into English in the essay "Seeking after the Connection from Differences — Pursuing the Beauty of Poems in the English Translation of Classical Chinese Poems"(*Foreign Language Research,* in the 4th issue, 1986). On this basis, as a further discussion, I wrote another paper entitled "On English Translation of Classical Chinese Poems" which was presented at the Symposium on Contemporary Translation in Hong Kong and later published (*Journal of Foreign Languages*, in the 4th issue, 1988). Both of the two papers attempted to stress the attention to culture in literary translation. This epilogue I am writing now still stresses the need for attention to culture in literary translation. Generally speaking, translation is cross-cultural. However, to be specific, literary translation is handling the symbols of two cultures as literature is the vehicle of a culture and the symbol of a culture as well.

Further, the translation of a poem is supposed to reach the readers in the target language and the target culture. These are the receptive subjects and their participation in the appreciation will turn the text of literary writing into literary works according to the theory of Reception Aesthetics (Hans Robert Jauss, 1967). If the translator ignores the fact that the readers, the receptive subjects, have grown up in a totally different culture, the translator's text remains opaque and will gain no appreciation from the receptive subjects at all. When they turn away from our translation and are reluctant or unable to participate in the final step in completing a creative work, the text of translation will miss the chance to become from text of translation to a piece of work of literary creation. Therefore, the translator fails in his task of introducing source-language poems into the target language and also blocks the way for the source-language poet to reach his readers in another culture.

Shadowed by this fear, I tried to figure out technically what I can do and what I can't. To be clearly aware of the limit of translation is the primary wisdom of a literary translator. Everything else, such as mastery of the two languages, knowledge in literature, skills in poetry writing, is all secondary. The purpose of translating classical Chinese poems is to introduce the ancient literary treasures with rich culture to English-speaking readers. The hope is to make it possible for readers to enjoy the poems and to enable them to experience the poetic excitement, enlightenment, transition from words to experience and the emotional satisfaction. These are what we can do through our efforts. Readers may even get interested in visiting China, in learning the Chinese language, and in touring those spots depicted in poems, all of which are also my concerns.

Now we can see the translator is tremendously trusted by the source-language poets, who do not know the target language, and also trusted by the target-language readers who do not know the source language. The cross-cultural communication totally relies on the translator who must be capable of handling the two languages and must be honest in dealing with the two parties and must make great efforts to find the spot between the two different cultures where he can get the connection for complete culture transcendence. It is crucial for the translator to be true, nothing but to be true.

Literary translators have to be true to the source-language poet. In the theory of Reception Aesthetics, the poet has been out of focus in the criticism of the poem. But for a poem translator, it is extremely important to know the poet's life well. This will enable the translator to reach the feeling of the poet and the unique emotion the poet put into a specific poem. The poet's personal life including his family, love, miseries, political setbacks and belonging to a certain school of style and so on, can be of help to access the meaning of the poem. Meaning is the most touching aspect of a poem. Sometimes it is accessible through implications of symbols, images, legends and mythology, which are usually hard to crack. If you know the poet well, you don't have to comprehend the poem based on your own assumptions. With complete comprehension as the basis, your translation will definitely be as appealing as the original.

The translators should feel that they are working with the poet or on behalf of the poet who may no longer be available to protect the text. The translators have to be sure of what the poet was trying to convey. Only with the understanding of what a poet trying to convey can a translator make the right choice from a range of ways. If the translators make inappropriate choice, the translators make the source-language poems sustain damage.

The translators have to be true to the original poem. No matter how hard it is, literary translators have to try their best to get the poetic meaning, the emotion, the insights, the cultural implications, images, symbols, allusive quotations and the tone of the poem. This is not merely a matter of rhetoric. It's my judgment that if we get these things done well, we are true to the poem and we are fair to the poet. No matter how inconvenient, we are supposed to exhaust our efforts to avoid, from the original poem, cutting off the key information, replacing elements, ignoring the allusive quotations or taking cultural implications for granted. As a literary translator, I never set up my own rules to confine the translation or to force the translation to fit a preconceive pattern. On the contrary, I tried to adjust myself to representing the original poem faithfully. I am willing to take the risk of being unable to justify my giving up the form of classical Chinese poems. It's my understanding that to transform the form of the classical Chinese poems into the form of English classical poems can only achieve the similarity to the form of classical Chinese poems. They can never be identical. However, similarity is not the same, not the genuine but unfortunately could be the counterfeit. I would give the form up rather than copy it with the scenario of damaged translation.

Classical Chinese poetry has its own metrical system which constrains strictly the length of each rhythmical line with the same number of words, the number of lines in a stanza and the number of stanzas in a poem. The system also has very strict patterns for musical effect: requiring words with a certain tone in a certain position in a certain line as there are four tones for words in Chinese and between every two neighboring lines requiring a pattern of antitheses in the tone of words in certain position. On top of that, between two certain parallel lines, words in the same position in each line have to be antitheses of each other in tone and in sense of both denotations and connotations. Nevertheless, they have to be the same part of speech and the same category of vocabulary. In addition to this, the two parallel lines of antitheses in the first four-line stanza have to be the third and the fourth lines; but the two parallel lines of antitheses in the second four-line stanza have to be the first and second lines. Further, between the last line in the first stanza and the first line of the second stanza, the pattern of antitheses in the tone of words is also applied. The requirement for rhyme is also strict. In an eight-line poem, the second line, the fourth line and the sixth line must be rhymed; in a four-line poem, the second line and the fourth line must be rhymed. This is a very complicated and impressive form cherished for almost one thousand five hundred years.

Actually, the exterior structure of the classical Chinese poems printed in this book has been shown in a very modern way. In ancient China, a poem was not written in short lines but just as a single piece similar to prose without any punctuation. And they were written in vertical way from top to bottom and moving for line change from right to left. The exterior of the classical Chinese poems printed in this book is already greatly altered, but it'll be received well because it suits the contemporary Chinese readers' reading habits, which, I can be sure, is what the target-language readers are used to. In the translation of classical Chinese poems, form can be dealt with as a superficial feature.

However, as time passed by, these patterns and rules were deserted in Chinese poetry composition in the early twentieth century. Since then Chinese poets have written free verse for almost a century. Why should we go back to the deserted form? I am not attempting to convey that to keep the form in English translation is an impossible mission but I am raising the flag about the issue that the vulnerability this type of translation causes to the meaning and imagination.

This type of desertion of the old metrical patterns and the old rhyming patterns also took place in English poetry. The world is changing all the time and the way we write poetry is changing, too. English poets began writing free verse about a hundred years ago due to the new poetry movement starting at the beginning of the twentieth century in the United States.

Free verse is not prose written in short lines but poetry with its own musical quality in each line. However, there is not a pattern to observe. I often read our English translation aloud to my co-translator John Knoepfle and he also read back to me aloud. And we listened to each other carefully to make sure the translation sounded appropriate as a poem. If it didn't, we would try again. We both enjoyed musical quality in each line though we are not following any preordained rhyme or meter. I hope that our English readers would like to read our translation aloud to enjoy the musical beauty of the free-verse translation. If so, I think we were true to the original poems.

Literary translators have to be true to the readers in the target language and target culture. The readers are in a way the patrons of the translator. It is common sense that the purpose of the translation is to make the source-language poem travel to another culture. The poem translated may sound foreign to the target-language readers, but it should be readable, acceptable, and attractive. The poems translated will be evaluated by readers of the target language, not by the translators. If readers there do not like them, the translation of the poems could not travel further.

Bearing this in mind, we are not bound to stay with the form of classical Chinese poems which is no longer in use and to copy the form into the form of the classical English poem which is no longer used either. The consequence of this process is likely to create a new poetic form which does not match the form of classical Chinese poems accurately and nor the form of classical English poem. We ought to know that whenever a form is deserted, it is obvious that readers have gotten tired of it. That's probably the only reason for the abandonment of the form of classical Chinese poems and the classical English poem. A translator has to know that to keep the form of the classical poems is nothing but an illusion that a dead form can survive.

Some translators go even further in presenting the form of classical Chinese poems by practicing omission, replacement, negligence, etc. to make it possible to get the original poem into the form the translator created. There is no doubt that in doing this the essence and the significance of the original poem will suffer. In some translations, omission, replacement and negligence simply take place to make the poem fit the form created by the translator — as if nothing had happened. Readers get no reminders, no explanations, no apology nor even a simple note. In cases like these, the translators abuse the power they have because the source-language poet relies on the translator and the target-language readers also rely on the translator. When the translator is confused by the situation thinking that he can do whatever he wants, he is trapped because there is always a large group of readers who know the target language, the source language and also the poems. They will be the aid of the readers in the target language. If we make this kind of mistake, we are not true to the readers because we are misleading them.

The rapport between the translator and the readers could be seriously damaged if the translator makes mistakes in the target language, because this can be considered even worse than a native speaker making a mistake in writing. Readers lose trust in the translators instead of forgiving them. Another factor that can also damage the rapport between the translator and the readers is missing information, especially missing cultural implications. Once this is found out by target-language readers, they will tend to come to the conclusion that the translator is not qualified because the translator doesn't even know the poem, the literature in his own language and culture.

Translators can never afford making mistakes in the target language and in culture of both the target language and the source language. We can do better if we never abuse the power of translators.

Literary translators have to be true to themselves. We have to be honest that we are not the poets. We are translating. Possibly we are poets, and we have even published poems, but we are not the poets who wrote the poems. We are translating. We must be sure we are not writing a poem but translating a poem. If we forget this, maybe just for a moment, the diction we select and the rhetoric we choose in translation will immediately betray our mission. Our mission is to get the meaning of the original poem accurately translated into the target language to inspire and thrill the readers of the target language and take them from words to experience. There are always various options of capacities of diction and rhetoric, which shape the unique individuality of the poet. A true translator chooses the capacity of diction and rhetoric to reflect the individuality for the source-language poet, absolutely not the individuality of the translators themselves.

True translators admit the limit of translation with no hesitation at all and also acknowledges their own limits in many aspects. Comparatively speaking, the latter is tougher. If we have this wisdom, then to gain the understanding of what we can't do and to gain the understanding of what we shouldn't do would both surely be easier. A translator's intuition must be able to sense the boundaries.

The most important thing for a true translator to closely follow and thoroughly explore is culture. The profound knowledge and exhaustive research of the two cultures will enable us enjoy the freedom to dance with them. If we can dance with cultures, we can make literary translation an extreme enjoyment and the enjoyment of free-dom in cross-cultural communication. To be bi-cultural seems as re-warding as to be bi-lingual.

To end this epilogue, I'd like to make it clear that all words written here come from my own experience in translating classical Chinese poems into English and the only intention of writing this is to share. I emphasized enhancing the attention, the reference to the culture and the recognition of culture in literary translation, but as we know literary translation is highly individual and somehow highly personal. It might occur to us, frankly speaking, as the proverb goes, that "one man's meat is another man's poison". Even so, it is always good to share a piece of information.

The pursuing of cultural approach in many subjects is well-recog-nized. It has been my understanding that literary translators have to be "culturally correct" instead of "technically correct". Professionals in many different cultures believe that a cultural approach is beneficial to their professions. When I worked on the English translation of classical Chinese poems, sometimes I felt at a loss, but I knew the bench marks were right there in the culture I was exposed to. Dancing with culture in translating classical Chinese poems is not only a matter of methodology but also a way for literary translators to escape from bondage.

No solution is perfect but I tried one which I believe works.

(Note: John Knoepfle has shared the same experience with me

through the collaboration and has been positive to all the thoughts and perspectives discussed in this epilogue.)

Wang Shouyi

Church Street, Toronto

September 4, 2017